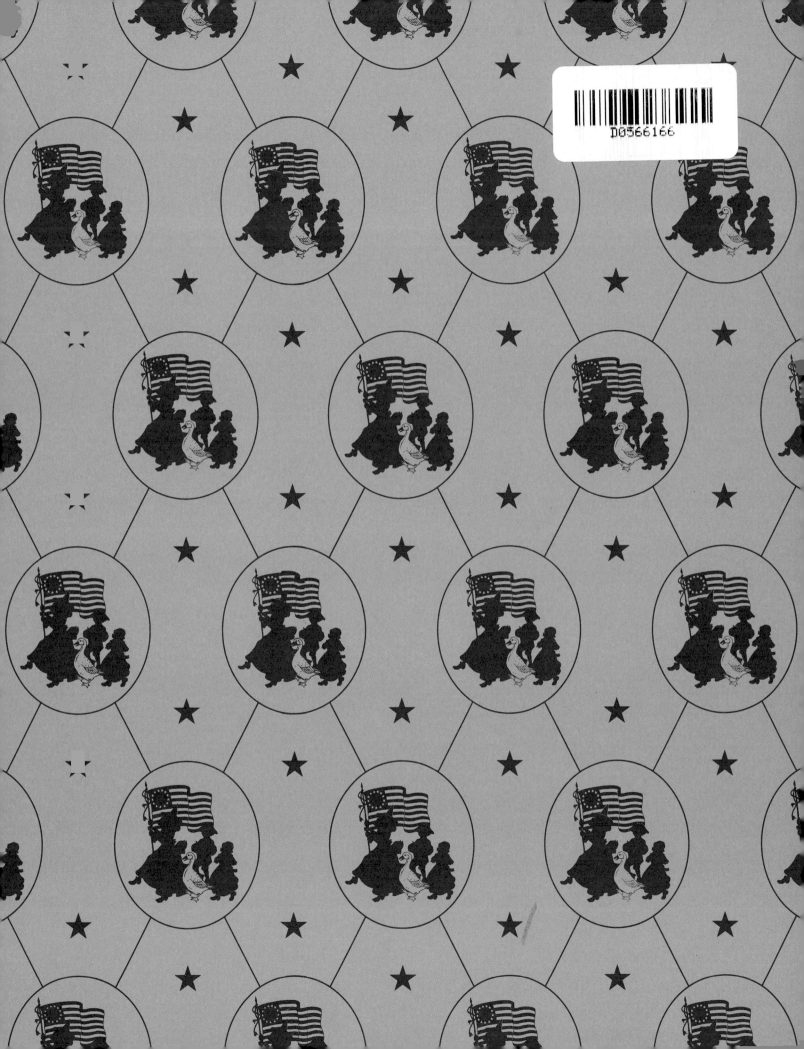

THE REAL
MOTHER GOOSE
BOOK OF
AMERICAN RHYMES

For Noonie, Poth, Cooks, and Chick,
without whom I would never have had a second chance at these rhymes.

THE REAL MOTHER GOOSE®

BOOK OF
AMERICAN
RHYMES

Selected by
Debby Slier

Illustrated by
Patty McCloskey-Padgett,
Bernice Loewenstein, Nan Pollard,
Cover art by Lynn Adams

SCHOLASTIC INC.
New York Toronto London Auckland Sydney
Mexico City New Delhi Hong Kong Buenos Aires

ACKNOWLEDGMENTS

Most of the rhymes in this book have been handed from generation to generation of children. Some of these rhymes originated in the Old World and were adapted by American children to make them their own. We are grateful to all children everywhere who have sung, jumped, or chanted these rhymes, and have thus kept them alive.

Every effort has been made to trace the ownership of all copyrighted material and to secure the necessary permissions to reprint these selections. In the event of any question arising as to the use of any material, the editor and the publisher, while expressing regret for any inadvertent error, will be happy to make the necessary correction in future printings.

Grateful acknowledgment is made to the following for permission to reprint the copyrighted material listed below:

Bantam Doubleday Dell for "Mice" from FIFTY-ONE NEW NURSERY RHYMES by Rose Fyleman. Copyright © 1931, 1932 by Doubleday, a division of Bantam Doubleday Dell Publishing Group, Inc. Used by permission of Doubleday, a division of Bantam Doubleday Dell Publishing Group, Inc.; "Miss White." From SHIMMY, SHIMMY, COKE-CA-POP by John Langstaff and Carol Langstaff. Copyright © 1973 by John Langstaff and Carol Langstaff. Illustrations © 1973 by Don MacSorley. Used by permission of Doubleday, a division of Bantam Doubleday Dell Publishing Group, Inc.; "Bedtime," from THE BUTTERFLY JAR by Jeff Moss. Copyright © 1989 by Jeff Moss. Used by permission of Bantam Books, a division of Bantam Doubleday Dell Publishing Group, Inc.

Kenneth C. Bennett for "A Modern Dragon" by Rowena Bennett. Reprinted by permission of Kenneth C. Bennett.

Gina Maccoby Literary Agency for "Ducks." From NUTS TO YOU AND NUTS TO ME by Mary Ann Hoberman. Copyright © 1974 by Mary Ann Hoberman. Reprinted by permission of Gina Maccoby Literary Agency; "The Folks Who Live in Backward Town." From HELLO AND GOOD-BYE by Mary Ann Hoberman. Copyright © 1959 by Mary Ann Hoberman. Reprinted by permission of Gina Maccoby Literary Agency.

HarperCollins for "Furry Ones" by Aileen Fisher from FEATHERED ONES AND FURRY. Reprinted by permission of HarperCollins; "Trains." From CRICKETY CRICKET! THE BEST LOVED POEMS OF JAMES S. TIPPETT by James Tippett. Copyright © 1933, copyright renewed 1973 by Martha K. Tippett. Selection reprinted by permission of HarperCollins Publishers.

Little, Brown and Company for "Notice." From ONE AT A TIME by David McCord. Copyright 1952 by David McCord. By permission of Little, Brown and Company; "Eletelephony." From TIRRA LIRRA: RHYMES OLD AND NEW by Laura E. Richards. Copyright © 1930, 1932 by Laura E. Richards. Copyright renewed 1960 by Hamilton Richards. By permission of Little, Brown and Company.

Macmillan Publishing Company for "New Moon." Reprinted with permission of Four Winds Press, an imprint of Macmillan Publishing Company, from THE HODGE PODGE BOOK, edited by Duncan Emrich. Copyright © 1972 by Duncan Emrich; Sailor Over the Sea" and "Betty Boop." Reprinted with permission of Four Winds Press, an imprint of Macmillan Publishing Company, from THE NONSENSE BOOK, edited by Duncan Emrich. Copyright © 1970 by Duncan Emrich; "The Little Turtle" by Vachel Lindsay. Reprinted with permission of Macmillan Publishing Company from COLLECTED POEMS OF VACHEL LINDSAY. Copyright © 1920 by Macmillan Publishing Company; renewed 1948 by Elizabeth C. Lindsay; "Monday Morning." Reprinted with permission of Macmillan Publishing Company from JUMP THE ROPE JINGLES by Emma Victor Worstell. Copyright © 1961 by Emma Victor Worstell.

John Travers Moore for "Kindness." From CERTAINLY, CARRIE, CUT THE CAKE by Margaret and John Travers Moore, copyright © 1971 by Margaret and John Travers Moore and published by the Bobbs Merrill Co. Permission to reprint by John Travers Moore.

Nina Payne for "Tag Along" by Nina Payne from ALL THE DAY LONG by Nina Payne. Copyright © 1973. Reprinted by permission of the author.

Professional Publishing Services for "Good Advice" by Louis Untermeyer from RAINBOW IN THE SKY Copyright © 1935. Reprinted by permission of the Estate of Louis Untermeyer, c/o Professional Publishing Services.

Anna Brooks Ramsay for "Poems" © 1993 by Anna Brooks Ramsay. Reprinted by permission of the author.

Random House for "Together." From EMBRACE: SELECTED LOVE POEMS by Paul Engle. Copyright © 1969 by Paul Engle. Reprinted by permission of Random House, Inc.

Scholastic, Inc. for "Holding Hands" by Lenore M. Link. Copyright © St. Nicholas Magazine. Reprinted by permission of Scholastic, Inc.

Zilpha Keatley Snyder for "Poem to Mud." Reprinted by permission of the author.

Jean Conder Soule for "Surprises." Used by permission of the author who retains all rights.

Clyde Watson for "Huckleberry, Gooseberry, Raspberry Pie." From FATHER FOX'S PENNYRHYMES published by Thomas Y. Crowell. Copyright © 1971. Reprinted by permission of Clyde Watson.

The poems in this book have been collected with the help of many people. We would particularly like to thank the librarians and staff at The American Anthropological Society; The American Folklife Center at the Library of Congress; The New York Public Library; The Texas Archives; and all the permissions managers at the various publishing houses who kindly searched their archives for us.

Book design by Tom Koken.

ISBN 0-439-63397-4

A LIST OF RHYMES

(For an alphabetical list of first lines see pp. 12-15)

A LIST OF RHYMES—Continued

A LIST OF FIRST LINES

OH MERRY MACK

Oh Merry Mack,
All dressed in black.
With silver buttons
All down her back.
She cannot read,
She cannot write.
But she can smoke
Her father's pipe.

GRACE

Grace, Grace,
All dressed in lace,
Went upstairs
To wash her face.

LOOBY LOO

Here we go looby loo,
Here we go looby light,
Here we go looby loo
All on a Saturday night.
Put your right hand in,
Put your right hand out,
Shake it a little, a little,
And turn yourself about.

DID YOU EVER

Did you ever, iver, over,
In your leefe, life, lofe,
See the devil, divil, dovel,
And his weefe, wife, wofe?

BOATS SAIL ON THE RIVERS

Boats sail on the rivers
    And ships sail on the sea;
But clouds that sail across the sky
    Are prettier far than these.

There are bridges on the rivers,
    As pretty as you please;
But the bow that bridges heaven,
    And overtops the trees,
And builds a road from earth to sky
    Is prettier far than these.

Christina Rossetti

ONE FOR SORROW

One for sorrow, two for joy,
Three for a girl, four for a boy,
Five for silver, six for gold,
Seven for a secret never to be told.

I OFTEN SIT AND WISH

I often sit and wish that I
Could be a kite up in the sky,
And ride upon the breeze and go
Whichever way I chanced to blow.

HOKEY POKEY

Hokey pokey, hanky panky,
I'm the king of Rankee-Jankee,
And I'm well, I thank yee.

ROBBIT AND BOBBIT

Robbit and Bobbit and big-bellied Ben
Could eat more meat than four score men;
Could eat a cow and a calf,
An ox and a half,
A church and a steeple,
And all the good people,
And then complain that his belly wasn't full.

OLD DAN TUCKER

Old Dan Tucker's come to town,
He swings the ladies round and round.
First to the east and then to the west,
And then to the one that he loves best.

Get out the way for old Dan Tucker,
Come too late to get his supper;
Supper's over and dishes washed.
And nothing's left but a piece of squash.

Old Dan Tucker is a fine old man.
Washed his face in a frying pan,
Combed his hair with a wagon wheel,
And died with a toothache in his heel.

AN OLD WOMAN

There was an old woman,
And she sold
Puddings and pies.
She went to the mill,
And the dust
Flew into her eyes.
Hot pies, and cold,
Pies to sell,
Wherever she goes,
You may follow her
By the smell.

WHEN I AM HUNGRY

I eat when I am hungry,
I drink when I am dry;
If a tree don't fall on me,
I'll live 'til I die.

MANNERS

Manners in the dining room,
Manners in the hall,
If you don't behave yourself,
You shall have none at all.

I EAT MY PEAS WITH HONEY

I eat my peas with honey,
I've done it all my life:
It makes the peas taste funny,
But it keeps them on my knife.

Gellette Burgess

TOM TEEPLE

Tom Teeple ate a steeple.
How could he do it, my good people?
I will tell you very plain,
Because it was made of sugar cane!

HAPPY IS THE MILLER

Happy is the miller
Who lives by himself,
All the bread and cheese
He piles upon the shelf,
One hand in the hopper,
And the other in the bag,
The wheel turns around
And he cries out, "Grab!"

GREGORY GRIGGS

Gregory Griggs, Gregory Griggs,
Had twenty-seven different wigs.
He wore them up;
He wore them down,
To please the people of the town;
He wore them east, he wore them west;
But he never could tell which he liked best.

CARRIE, CUT THE CAKE

Certainly Carrie, cut the cake—
Cut it carefully, goodness' sake:
Cherries for the children,
Chestnuts (a few),
And chocolate,
Just for you!

19

THE DERBY RAM

As I was going to Derby,
Upon a market day,
I saw the biggest ram, sir,
That ever was fed with hay.

The ram that was in Derby,
As all have heard it said,
He was the biggest ram, sir,
That ever wore a head.

The ram was fat behind, sir,
The ram was fat before,
He measured ten yards round, sir,
I think it was no more.

The ram he had four feet, sir,
He had four feet to stand,
And every track he made, sir,
It covered an acre of land.

The man that fed the ram, sir
He fed him twice a day,
And each time that he fed him,
He ate a rick of hay.

The wool grew on his back, sir,
It reached to the sky.
And there the eagles built their nests,
I heard the young one's cry.

The wool on this ram's flanks, sir,
It dragged on to the ground,
The Devil cut it off, sir,
To make himself a gown.

The wool upon his tail, sir,
Filled more than fifty bags,
You'd better keep away, sir,
When that tail shakes and wags.

The wool upon his tail, sir,
Was very fine and thin,
Took all the girls of Derby Town,
Full seven years to spin.

The ram it had two horns, sir,
That reach-ed to the moon,
A man went up in December,
And never came down till June.

The space between his horns, sir,
'Twas more than a man could reach,
And there they built a pulpit, sir,
The parson there to preach.

And if you think "not so," sir,
If you should think I lie,
Oh you go down to Derby, sir,
And you'll see same as I.

BETTY BOOP

Betty Boop—
Isn't she cute?
All she eats is
Vegetable soup.

MABEL, MABEL

Mabel, Mabel strong and able,
Take your elbows off the table.
We've told you once,
We've told you twice,
We'll never tell you thrice.

CRY BABY

Cry baby, cry.
Stick your finger in your eye,
And tell your mama it wasn't I.

MY LITTLE SISTER

My little sister
Likes to eat,
But when she does
She's not too neat.
The trouble is
She doesn't know
Exactly where
The food should go!

William Wise

THE GOOPS

The Goops they lick their fingers,
    And the Goops they lick their knives;
They spill their broth on the tablecloth—
    Oh, they lead disgusting lives!
The goops they talk while eating,
    And loud and fast they chew;
And that is why I'm glad that I
    Am not a Goop—are you?

Gelett Burgess

22

MISS WHITE

Miss White had a fight
In the middle of the night.
She saw a ghost eating toast
Halfway up the lamppost.

John and Carol Langstaff

JOE, JOE

Joe, Joe, stubbed his toe
On the way to Mexico.
On the way back,
He hurt his back,
Sliding on the railroad track.

Frank, Frank,
Turned the crank,
His Mother came out
And gave him a spank.

Bert, Bert, tore his shirt
Riding on a lump of dirt.

JEREMIAH

Jeremiah, blow the fire.
Puff, puff, puff.
Jeremiah, blow the fire.
Puff, puff, puff.
First you blow it gently,
Then you blow it rough.

THE POOR WIDOW

There comes a poor widow from
    Cumberland,
With all her poor children in her hand;
One can brew, and one can bake,
And one can make a wedding cake.

CHARLEY, CHARLEY

Charley, Charley, stole some barley
Out of the baker's shop.
The baker came out
And gave him a clout,
And Charley went out hop, hop, hop.

JOHNNY

Johnny on the woodpile,
Johnny on the fence.
Johnny got a haircut
For fifteen cents.

OLD MacDONALD

Old MacDonald had a farm,
E - I - E - I - 0.
And on this farm he had some sheep,
E - I - E - I - 0.
With a baa-baa here and a baa-baa there,
Here a baa, there a baa, ev'rywhere a baa-baa.

Old MacDonald had a farm,
E - I - E - I - 0.
And on this farm he had some cows,
E - I - E - I - 0.
With a moo-moo here and a moo-moo there,
Here a moo, there a moo, ev'rywhere a moo-moo.

Old MacDonald had a farm,
E - I - E - I - 0.
And on this farm he had some chicks,
E - I - E - I - 0.
With a chick-chick here and a chick-chick there,
Here a chick, there a chick, ev'rywhere a chick-chick.

Old MacDonald had a farm,
E - I - E - I - 0.
And on this farm he had some ducks,
E - I - E - I - 0.
With a quack-quack here, and a quack-quack there,
Here a quack, there a quack, ev'rywhere a quack-quack.

Old MacDonald had a farm,
E - I - E - I - 0.
And on this farm he had some donkeys,
E - I - E - I - 0.
With a hee-haw here and a hee-haw there,
Here a hee, there a haw, ev'rywhere a hee-haw.

Old MacDonald had a farm,
E - I - E - I - 0.
And on this farm he had some cats,
E - I - E - I - 0.
With a meow-meow here and a meow-meow there,
Here a meow, there a meow, ev'rywhere a meow-meow.

Old MacDonald had a farm,
E - I - E - I - 0.
And on this farm he had some dogs,
E - I - E - I - 0.
With a woof-woof here and a woof-woof there,
Here a woof, there a woof, ev'rywhere a woof-woof.

Old MacDonald had a farm
E - I - E - I - 0.
And on this farm he had some pigs,
E - I - E - I - 0.
With an oink-oink here and an oink-oink there,
Here an oink, there an oink, ev'rywhere an oink-oink.
E-I, E-I, -O-O-O-O.

STAR LIGHT, STAR BRIGHT

Star light, star bright,
First star I see tonight,
I wish I may, I wish I might
Have the wish I wish tonight.

THE STAR

Twinkle, twinkle, little star,
How I wonder what you are!
Up above the world so high,
Like a diamond in the sky.

When the blazing sun is set,
And the grass with dew is wet,
Then you show your little light,
Twinkle, twinkle, all the night.

Then the traveler in the dark,
Thanks you for your tiny spark,
He could not see where to go
If you did not twinkle so.

In the dark blue sky you keep,
And often through my curtains peep,
For you never shut your eye
Till the sun is in the sky.

As your bright and tiny spark
Lights the traveler in the dark,
Though I know not what you are,
Twinkle, twinkle, little star.

Jane Taylor

QUAKER, QUAKER

"Quaker, Quaker, how art thee?"
"Very well, I thank thee."
"How's thy neighbor, next to thee?"
"I don't know, but I'll go see."

DOCTOR, DON'T YOU CRY

Doctor, doctor, don't you cry!
Your true love will soon come by.
If she comes all dressed in green,
That's a sign she's to be seen.
If she comes all dressed in white,
That's a sign she'll cry all night.
If she comes all dressed in gray,
That's a sign that she's away.
If she comes all dressed in blue,
That's the sign she'll marry you.

MR. NOBODY

I know a funny little man,
    As quiet as a mouse,
Who does the mischief that is done
    In everybody's house!
There's no one ever sees his face,
    And yet we all agree
That every plate we broke was cracked
    By Mr. Nobody.
'Tis he who always tears our books,
    Who leaves the door ajar,
He pulls the buttons from our shirts,
    And scatters pins afar;
That squeaking door will always squeak,
    For, prithee, don't you see,
We leave the oiling to be done
    By Mr. Nobody.

The fingermarks upon the door
    By none of us are made,
We never leave the blinds unclosed,
    To let the curtains fade.
The ink we never spill; the boots
    That lying around you see
Are not our boots—they all belong
    To Mr. Nobody.

ONE, TWO, THREE, FOUR

One, two, three, four—
Preacher's at the chapel door.
Five, six, seven, eight—
Wonder who will come in late.
In comes Cat, in comes Rat,
In comes the lady with the great big hat.

WHAT'S YOUR NAME?

What's your name?
Puddin Tame.
Ask me again
And I'll tell you the same.
Where do you live?
In a sieve.
What's your number?
Cucumber!

SURPRISES

Surprises are round
     Or long and tallish.
Surprises are square
     Or flat and smallish.

Surprises are wrapped
     With paper and bow,
And hidden in closets
     Where secrets won't show.

Surprises are often
     Good things to eat;
A get-well toy or
     A birthday treat.

Surprises come
     In such interesting sizes—
I LIKE
     SURPRISES!

Jean Conder Soule

MRS. DAY

Mrs. Day made a cake,
The cake was soggy.
She fed it to her doggy.
The doggy ate the cake
And got a stomach ache.

LITTLE ORPHAN ANNIE

Little Orphan Annie
Sitting in the sun,
Had a piece of baloney,
And wouldn't give me none.
Take a bite, take a bite,
It's good for your appetite.

MOTHER, MOTHER

Mother, Mother, pin a rose on me.
Two little boys are after me.
One is blind, and the other can't see.
Mother, Mother, pin a rose on me.

I CLIMBED UP THE APPLE TREE

I climbed up the apple tree
And all the apples fell on me.
Make a pudding, make a pie.
Did you ever tell a lie?
Yes, you did, you know you did.
You stole your mother's teapot lid.

SMARTY, SMARTY

Smarty, Smarty,
Gave a party—
Nobody came.

Smarty, Smarty,
Gave another party—
Just the same.

KINDNESS

A kettle's for the kitchen,
A key is for the door,
A kitten is for playing with
And keeping on the floor.

A kite is made for flying
When March winds blow,
Kindness is for everyone—
Didn't you know?

Margaret and John Travers Moore

JACK HALL

Jack Hall,
He is so small,
A mouse could eat him,
Hat and all.

MICE

I think mice
Are rather nice,
Their tails are long,
Their faces small,
They haven't any
Chins at all.
Their ears are pink,
Their teeth are white,
They run about
The house at night.
They nibble things
They shouldn't touch
And no one seems
To like them much.

But I think mice
Are nice.

Rose Fyleman

TEN LITTLE MICE

Ten little mice sat in a barn to spin,
Pussy came by and popped her head in:
What are you at, my jolly ten?
We're making coats for gentlemen.
Shall I come in and cut your threads?
No, Miss Puss, you'd bite off our heads.

THE GIANT JIM

The giant Jim, great giant Jim,
Wears a hat without a brim,
Weighs a ton, and wears a blouse,
And trembles when he meets a mouse.

THREE LITTLE MICE

Three little mice ran up the stairs
To hear their teacher say her prayers.
When the teacher said, "Amen,"
The three little mice ran down again.

THE CITY MOUSE

The city mouse lives in a house;
    The garden mouse lives in a bower,
He's friendly with the frogs and toads,
    And sees the pretty plants in flower.

The city mouse eats bread and cheese;
    The garden mouse eats what he can;
We will not grudge him seeds and stalks.
    Poor little timid furry man.

Christina Rossetti

THE JUMBLIES

They went to sea in a Sieve, they did,
  In a Sieve they went to sea;
In spite of all their friends could say,
On a winter's morn, on a stormy day,
  In a Sieve they went to sea!
And when the Sieve turned round and round,
And everyone cried, "You'll all be drowned!"
They called aloud, "Our Sieve ain't big,
But we don't care a button! We don't care a fig!
  In a Sieve we'll go to sea!"
    Far and few, far and few,
      Are the lands where the Jumblies live;
     Their heads are green, and their hands are blue,
     And they went to sea in a Sieve.

They sailed away in a Sieve, they did,
  In a Sieve they sailed so fast,
With only a beautiful pea-green veil
Tied with a riband by way of a sail,
  To a small tobacco-pipe mast;
And everyone said, who saw them go,
"O won't they be soon upset, you know!
For the sky is dark, and the voyage is long,
And happen what may, it's extremely wrong
  In a Sieve to sail so fast!"
    Far and few, far and few,
      Are the lands where the Jumblies live;
     Their heads are green, and their hands are blue,
     And they went to sea in a Sieve.

The water it soon came in, it did,
  The water it soon came in;
So to keep them dry, they wrapped their feet
In a pinky paper all folded neat,
  And they fastened it down with a pin.
And they passed the night in a crockery-jar,
And each of them said, "How wise we are!
Though the sky be dark, and the voyage be long,
Yet we never can think we were rash or wrong,
  While round in our Sieve we spin!"
    Far and few, far and few,
      Are the lands where the Jumblies live;
    Their heads are green, and their hands are blue,
      And they went to sea in a Sieve.

And all night long they sailed away;
  And when the sun went down,
They whistled and warbled a moony song
To the echoing sound of a coppery gong,
  In the shade of the mountains brown.
"O Timballoo! How happy we are,
When we live in a Sieve and a crockery-jar,
And all night long in the moonlight pale,
We sail away with a pea-green sail,
  In the shade of the mountains brown!"
    Far and few, far and few,
      Are the lands where the Jumblies live;
    Their heads are green, and their hands are blue,
      And they went to sea in a Sieve.

33

They sailed to the Western Sea, they did,
　To a land all covered with trees;
And they bought an owl, and a useful cart,
And a pound of rice, and a cranberry-tart,
　And a hive of silvery bees;
And they bought a pig, and some green jackdaws,
And a lovely monkey with lollipop paws,
And forty bottles of ring-bo-ree,
　And no end of Stilton cheese.
　　Far and few, far and few,
　　　Are the lands where the Jumblies live;
　　Their heads are green, and their hands are blue,
　　　And they went to sea in a Sieve.

And in twenty years they all came back,
　In twenty years or more;
And everyone said, "How tall they've grown!
For they've been to the Lakes, and the Torrible Zone
　And the hills of the Chankly Bore."
And they drank their health, and gave them a feast
Of dumplings made of beautiful yeast;
And everyone said, "If we only live,
We, too, will go to sea in a Sieve,
　To the hills of the Chankly Bore."
　　Far and few, far and few,
　　　Are the lands where the Jumblies live;
　　Their heads are green, and their hands are blue,
　　　And they went to sea in a Sieve.

Edward Lear

34

JUMP

Jump—jump—jump—
　　Jump away
From this town into
　　The next, today.

Jump—jump—jump—
　　Jump over the moon;
Jump all the morning,
　　And all the noon.

Jump—jump—jump—
　　Jump all night;
Won't our mothers
　　Be in a fright?

Jump—jump—jump—
　　Over the sea;
What wonderful wonders
　　We shall see.

Jump—jump—jump—
　　Jump far away;
And all come home
　　Some other day.

Kate Greenaway

OPEN YOUR MOUTH

Open your mouth
And close your eyes.
And you will get
A big surprise.

MISTER RABBIT

Mister Rabbit, Mister Rabbit,
　　Your ears are mighty long.
　　Yes, my friend,
　　　　They're put on wrong!

Mister Rabbit, Mister Rabbit,
　　Your coat's mighty gray.
　　Yes, my friend,
　　　　'Twas made that way!

Mister Rabbit, Mister Rabbit,
　　Your feet are mighty red.
　　Yes, my friend,
　　　　I'm almost dead!

Mister Rabbit, Mister Rabbit,
　　Your tail's mighty white.
　　Yes, my friend,
　　　　And I'm getting
Out of sight!

THE BEAR WENT OVER THE MOUNTAIN

The bear went over the mountain,
The bear went over the mountain,
The bear went over the mountain,
And what do you think he saw?

A valley in the mountain,(three times)
Then what do you think he saw?

A river in the valley,(three times)
Then what do you think he saw?

A boat on the river, (three times)
Then what do you think he saw?

A house on the boat, (three times)
Then what do you think he saw?

A man in the house, (three times)
Then what do you think he saw?

Pants on the man, (three times)
Then what do you think he saw?

Pocket in the pants, (three times)
Then what do you think he saw?

A nickel in the pocket, (three times)
Then what do you think he saw?

A buffalo on the nickel, (three times)
Then what do you think he saw?

Hair on the buffalo, (three times)
Then what do you think he saw?

A cootie in the hair, (three times)
Then what do you think he saw?

Glasses on the cootie, (three times)
Then what do you think he saw?

A crack in the glass, (three times)
Then what do you think he saw?

Water in the crack, (three times)
Then what do you think he saw?

Dirt in the water, (three times)
Then what do you think he saw?

NOTHING!

SLINGSHOT HARRY

Slingshot Harry
Went and shot a bear,
Shot him full of buckshot,
And never touched a hair.

THE SILLY OWL

In an old oak there lived an owl,
　　Frisky, whisky, wheedle.
She thought herself a clever fowl,
　　Fiddle faddle feedle.

Her face alone her wisdom shew,
　　Frisky, whisky, wheedle!
For all she said was: Whit to whoo!
　　Fiddle, faddle, feedle!

Her silly note a gunner heard,
　　Frisky, whisky, wheedle!
Says he, I'll shoot you, stupid bird!
　　Fiddle, faddle, feedle!

Now if he'd not heard her hoot,
　　Frisky, whisky, wheedle!
He'd not found her out to shoot,
　　Fiddle, faddle, feedle!

CHICKENS

Said the first little chicken,
　　With a queer little squirm,
"I wish I could find
　　A fat little worm!"

Said the next little chicken,
　　With an odd little shrug,
"I wish I could find
　　A fat little bug!"

Said the third little chicken,
　　With a small sigh of grief,
"I wish I could find
　　A green little leaf!"

Said the fourth little chicken,
　　With a faint little moan,
"I wish I could find
　　A wee gravel stone!"

"Now see here!" said the mother,
　　From the green garden patch,
"If you want any breakfast,
　　Just come here and scratch!"

37

THE WIND

I come to work as well as play;
    I'll tell you what I do;
I whistle all the live-long day,
    "Woo-oo-oo-oo! Woo-oo!"

I toss the branches up and down
    And shake them to and fro,
I whirl the leaves in flocks of brown,
    And send them high and low.

I strew the twigs upon the ground,
    The frozen earth I sweep;
I blow the children round and round
    And wake the flowers from sleep.

RAIN

The rain is raining all around,
It falls on field and tree,
It rains on the umbrellas here,
And on the ships at sea.

Robert Louis Stevenson

IT'S RAINING, IT'S POURING

It's raining, it's pouring,
The old man is snoring;
He got into bed with a bump on
    his head,
And didn't get up in the morning.

MACKEREL SKY

Mackerel sky,
Mackerel sky,
Never long wet,
And never long dry.

RAIN, RAIN

Rain, rain, go away.
Come again another day.
Little Johnny wants to play.

SEASON SONG

Spring is showery, flowery, bowery.
Summer is hoppy, croppy, poppy.
Autumn is wheezy, sneezy, freezy.
Winter is slippy, drippy, nippy.

EENCY, WEENCY, SPIDER

Eency, Weency, spider went up
    the water spout.
Down came the rain and washed
    poor Eency Weency out.
Out came the sun and dried up
    all the rain.
So Eency, Weency spider climbed
    up the spout again.

CINDERELLA

Cinderella, dressed in yella,
Went upstairs to kiss a fella.
Made a mistake and kissed a snake.
How many doctors did it take?

I'M GLAD

I'm glad the sky is painted blue,
    And the earth is painted green,
With such a lot of nice fresh air
    All sandwiched in between.

POEMS

Poems, poems everywhere
In my mind and in my hair
Poems, poems all around
Oops!
I dropped one on the ground.
Writing poems is my joy
Finishing one is like a new toy
The end of a sentence
Has a nice rhyme
And poems never waste my time.

Poems, poems everywhere
Some in my lap
And some over there!

Anna Brooks Ramsey

WHOLE DUTY OF CHILDREN

A child should always say what's true
And speak when he is spoken to,
And behave mannerly at table;
At least as far as he is able.

Robert Louis Stevenson

ALL GOOD CHILDREN

One, two, three, four, five, six, seven,
All good children go to heaven.
When they die, they say good-bye.
One, two, three, four, five, six, seven.

MONKEY ON THE RAILROAD

Monkey on the railroad,
Monkey on the fence,
Monkey get your hair cut—
Fifteen cents.
Monkey in the barnyard,
Monkey in the stable,
Monkey get your hair cut
Soon as you are able.

I KNOW SOMETHING

I know something I won't tell;
Three little monkeys in a peanut shell.
One can read and one can write,
And one can smoke a corncob pipe.

WELL I NEVER

Well I never, did you ever,
See a monkey dressed in leather?
Leather eyes,
Leather nose,
Leather breeches to his toes.

ONCE UPON A TIME

Once upon a time
A monkey drank some wine,
Then he danced a jig on the
streetcar line.

The streetcar broke,
The monkey choked,
Then he went to heaven in a
little tin boat.

POP! GOES THE WEASEL

All around the cobbler's bench
The monkey chased the weasel.
The monkey thought 'twas all in fun—
Pop! goes the weasel.

Johnny has the whooping cough
Mary has the measles.
That's the way the money goes—
Pop! goes the weasel.

A penny for a spool of thread,
A penny for a needle,
That's the way the money goes—
Pop! goes the weasel.

Every time that I go out,
The monkey's on the table,
Take a stick and knock him off—
Pop! goes the weasel.

THE DUEL

The gingham dog and the calico cat
Side by side on the table sat;
'Twas half-past twelve, and (what do you think)
Nor one nor t' other had slept a wink!
  The old Dutch clock and the Chinese plate
  Appeared to know as sure as fate
There was going to be a terrible spat.
  (I wasn't there; I simply state
  What was told to me by the Chinese plate!)

The gingham dog went, "bow-wow-wow"
And the calico cat replied, "mee-ow!"
The air was littered, an hour or so,
With bits of gingham and calico,
  While the old Dutch clock in the chimney-place
  Up with its hands before its face,
For it always dreaded a family row.
  (Now mind: I'm only telling you
  What the old Dutch clock declares is true!)

The Chinese plate looked very blue,
And wailed, "Oh, dear! what shall we do!"
But the gingham dog and the calico cat
Wallowed this way and tumbled that,
    Employing every tooth and claw
    In the awfulest way you ever saw—
And, oh! how the gingham and calico flew!
    (Don't fancy I exaggerate—
    I got my news from the Chinese plate!)

Next morning, where the two had sat
They found no trace of dog or cat—
And some folks think unto this day
That burglars stole that pair away!
    But the truth about the cat and pup
    Is this: they ate each other up!
Now what do you really think of that!
    (The old Dutch clock it told me so,
    And that is how I came to know.)

Eugene Field

TAG ALONG

Sing song
Tag along
Standing by the wall.

Crank pot
Whine a lot
Just because you're small.

Big shot
Red hot
Go and wilt a flower.

Rough tough
Mean enough
To make the milk sour.

Nina Payne

LIFE IS LIKE A ROSE

Life is like a rose,
Life is like a blossom.
If you want your finger bit,
Stick it at a possum.

NEEDLE TO NEEDLE

Needle to needle, stitch to stitch,
Pull the old woman out of the ditch,
If you ain't out by the time I'm in,
I'll wrap your knuckles with my
    knitting pin.

I HAD A LITTLE BROTHER

I had a little brother,
His name was Tiny Tim.
I put him in the bathtub
To teach him how to swim.
He drank up all the water,
He ate up all the soap.
He died last night
With a bubble in his throat.

OVER THE HILLS

Over the hills and a good way off,
A woodchuck died of the
    whooping-cough.
The thunders rolled, and the
    lightnings flashed,
And broke Grandma's teapot
    all to smash.

VIRGINIA HAD A BABY

Virginia had a baby;
She named him Tiny Tim;
She put him in the bathtub
To teach him how to swim.
He floated up the river;
He floated down the lake;
Now Virginia's baby
Has got a stomachache.

TEDDY ON THE RAILROAD

Teddy on the railroad,
Picking up stones;
Along came an engine
And broke all Teddy's bones.
"Oh," said Teddy,
"That's no fair!"
"Oh," said the engineer,
"I don't care."

WHERE SHALL
I FIND HER?

It's raining,
It's hailing,
A cold frosty
    morning,
In steps
    the farmer,
A-drinking of
    the cider,
I'll be
    the reaper,
You'll be
    the binder,
I lost my
    true love,
And where shall
    I find her?

FROG WENT A-COURTING

Mr. Froggie went a-courting and he did ride;
Sword and pistol by his side.

He went to Mrs. Mousie's hall,
Gave a loud knock and gave a loud call.

"Pray, Mrs. Mousie, are you within?"
"Yes, kind sir, I sit and spin."

He took Miss Mousie on his knee,
And said, "Miss Mousie, will you marry me?"

Miss Mousie blushed and hung her head,
"You'll have to ask Uncle Rat," she said.

"Not without Uncle Rat's consent,
Would I marry the President."

Uncle Rat jumped up and shook his fat side,
To think his niece would be Bill Frog's bride.

Next day Uncle Rat went to town,
To get his niece a wedding gown.

Where shall the wedding supper be?
'Way down yonder in a hollow tree.

First come in was a Bumble-bee,
Who danced a jig with Captain Flea.

Next come in was a Butterfly,
Selling butter very high.

And when they all set down to sup,
A big gray goose came and gobbled them all up.

And this is the end of one, two, three,
The Rat and the Mouse and the little Froggie.

ONE DAY WHEN I WAS WALKING

One day when I was walking
I heard my boyfriend talking
To the pretty girl
With the strawberry curl.
And this is what he said,
"I love you."
She jumped in the lake
And swallowed a snake
And came back with a bellyache.

I SHOULD WORRY

I should worry,
I should care,
I should marry a millionaire;
Should he die, I would cry—
Then I'd marry a richer guy.

HERE COMES THE BRIDE

Here comes the bride
All dressed in white.
See how she wobbles
From side to side.

I LOVE MY WIFE

I love my wife, I love my baby.
I love my biscuits sopped in gravy.

ONE, I LOVE

One, I love,
Two, I love,
Three, I love, I say,
Four, I love with all my heart,
And five, I cast away;
Six, he loves,
Seven, she loves,
Eight, they both love;
Nine, he comes,
Ten, he tarries,
Eleven, he courts,
Twelve, he marries;
Thirteen, wishes,
Fourteen, kisses,
All the rest little witches.

HUSH, LITTLE BABY

Hush, little baby, don't say a word,
Papa's gonna buy you a mockingbird.

And if that mockingbird won't sing,
Papa's gonna buy you a diamond ring.

And if that diamond ring turns to
    brass,
Papa's gonna buy you a looking glass.

And if that looking glass gets broke,
Papa's gonna buy you a billy goat.

And if that billy goat won't pull,
Papa's gonna buy you a cart and bull.

And if that cart and bull turn over,
Papa's gonna buy you a dog named
    Rover.
And if that dog named Rover won't
    bark,
Papa's gonna buy you a horse and cart.

And if that horse and cart fall down,
You'll still be the sweetest little baby
    in town.

IBBITY, BIBBITY

Ibbity, bibbity, sibbity, sa
Ibbity, bibbity, vanilla.
Down the ferry, fun, fun, fun.
Eighteen hundred and ninety-one.

HUSHABYE

Hushabye,
Don't you cry,
Go to sleep, little baby.
When you wake I'll give you cake
And lots of pretty horses.
One will be red,
One will be blue,
One will be the color of
Mammy's shoe.
Hushabye,
Don't you cry,
Go to sleepy, little baby

FUDGE

Fudge—Fudge—call the judge,
Mother has a brand-new baby.
    It's not a girl,
    It's not a boy,
It's just a newborn baby.
Wrap it up in tissue paper,
Put it in the elevator.

BLACKBIRD

Blackbird whistle, woodpecker drum,
"Spring has come, Spring has come."
Cardinal sing in the maple tree,
"Spring is here for you and me."
Longer day and shorter night,
Little boy, bring out your kite.

GOOD ADVICE

Don't shirk
Your work
For the sake of a dream;
A fish
In a dish
Is worth ten in a stream.

Louis Untermeyer

TOGETHER

Because we do
All things together
All things improve,
Even weather.

Our daily meat
And bread taste better,
Trees are greener
Rain is wetter.

Paul Engle

THE SWING

How do you like to go up in a swing,
Up in the air so blue?
Oh, I do think it is the pleasantest thing
Ever a child can do!

Up in the air and over the wall,
Till I can see so wide,
Rivers and trees and cattle and all
Over the countryside—

Till I look down on the garden green,
Down on the roof so brown—
Up in the air I go flying again,
Up in the air and down!

Robert Louis Stevenson

THE WORLD

The world is so full of a number
of things,
I'm sure we should all be as
happy as kings.

Robert Louis Stevenson

LITTLE WIND

Little wind, blow on the hilltop,
Little wind, blow in the plain;
Little wind, blow up the sunshine,
Little wind, blow off the rain.

Kate Greenaway

MOTHER MOREY

I'll tell you a story
About old Mother Morey,
And now my story's begun;
I'll tell you another
About her brother,
And now my story is done.

QUEEN CAROLINE

Queen, Queen Caroline,
Dipped her hair in turpentine;
Turpentine made it shine,
Queen, Queen Caroline.

ROSES ARE RED

Roses are red,
Violets are blue,
Sugar is sweet,
And so are you.

LAVENDER'S BLUE

Lavender's blue, diddle, diddle,
Lavender's green;

When I am king, diddle, diddle,
You shall be queen.

Call up your men, diddle, diddle,
Set them to work,

Some to the plow, diddle, diddle,
Some to the cart.

Some to make hay, diddle, diddle,
Some to cut corn,

While you and I, diddle, diddle,
Keep ourselves warm.

THERE WAS AN OLD LADY

There was an old lady, she swallowed a fly.
I don't know why she swallowed a fly.
Perhaps she'll die.

There was an old lady, she swallowed a spider.
It wriggled and jiggled and tickled inside her.
She swallowed the spider to catch the fly.
I don't know why she swallowed a fly.
Perhaps she'll die.

There was an old lady, she swallowed a bird.
How absurd! She swallowed a bird.
She swallowed the bird to catch the spider,
She swallowed the spider to catch the fly,
I don't know why she swallowed a fly.
Perhaps she'll die.

There was an old lady, she swallowed a cat.
Fancy that! She swallowed a cat.
She swallowed the cat to catch the bird.
She swallowed the bird to catch the spider,
She swallowed the spider to catch the fly,
I don't know why she swallowed a fly.
I think she'll die.

There was an old lady, she swallowed a dog.
She went the whole hog, she swallowed the dog.
She swallowed the dog to catch the cat,
She swallowed the cat to catch the bird,
She swallowed the bird to catch the spider.
She swallowed the spider to catch the fly,
I don't know why she swallowed a fly.
Perhaps she'll die.

There was an old lady, she swallowed a cow.
I don't know how she swallowed the cow.
She swallowed the cow to catch the dog,
She swallowed the dog to catch the cat,
She swallowed the cat to catch the bird,
She swallowed the bird to catch the spider,
She swallowed the spider to catch the fly,
I don't know why she swallowed a fly.
Perhaps she'll die.

There was an old lady, she swallowed a horse.   She died, of course.

THANKSGIVING DAY

Over the river and through the wood,
To grandfather's house we go;
The horse knows the way
To carry the sleigh
Through the white and drifted snow.

Over the river and through the wood—
Oh, how the wind does blow!
It stings the toes
And bites the nose,
As over the ground we go.

Over the river and through the wood,
To have a first-rate play.
Hear the bells ring,
"Ting-a-ling-ding!"
Hurrah for Thanksgiving Day!

Over the river and through the wood
Trot fast, my dapple-gray!
Spring over the ground,
Like a hunting-hound!
For this is Thanksgiving Day.

Over the river and through the wood,
And straight through the barnyard gate.
We seem to go
Extremely slow,—
It is so hard to wait!

Over the river and through the wood—
Now grandmother's cap I spy!
Hurrah for the fun!
Is the pudding done?
Hurrah for the pumpkin-pie!

Lydia Maria Child

ME, MYSELF, AND I

Me, myself, and I—
We went to the kitchen and ate a pie.
Then my mother, she came in
And chased us out with a rolling pin.

MY MOTHER AND YOUR MOTHER

My mother and your mother
Were hanging out the clothes;
My mother hit your mother on the
    nose.
What color blood came out?
R E D spells RED.

I ASKED MY MOTHER FOR FIFTY CENTS

I asked my mother for fifty cents
To see the elephant jump the fence.
He jumped so high,
He touched the sky,
And never came back until the Fourth
    of July.

I asked my mother for more.
To see the elephant climb the door.
He jumped so low,
He bumped his toe,
And that was the end of the
    elephant show.

MY MOTHER

My mother and your mother
Live across the way.
Every time they have a fight,
This is what they say:
Ickabocker, ickabocker,
    ickabocker, boo!
Ickabocker, soda cracker,
    out goes you!

TWO LITTLE TOADIES

Two little toadies went out for a walk,
And arm and arm they had a nice talk.

When they were many miles from home,
Each sat down on a dusty stone,
Till the stars came out and they felt afraid,
For they saw an old owl sitting in state
And then they knew it was getting late.

Then Specklety to his brother said,
"I've a fearful pain in my head,
I almost wish that I were dead."

Then each took turns to carry the other,
Specklety first and then his brother.

And when they reached home, each one said,
"In a burdock leaf I will cool my head."

Then each little toady tucked in his toes,
And lay in the rushes till the moon rose.

Then the lily-bells chimed in the pale moonlight,
And the birds all whispered,
    "Good-night, Good-night."

FIVE LITTLE SQUIRRELS

Five little squirrels sat up in a tree.
The first one said, "What do I see?"
The second one said, "A man with a gun."
The third one said, "Then we'd better run."
The fourth one said, "Let's hide in the shade."
Then BANG went the gun, and how they did run.

SQUIRREL

Whisky, frisky,
Hippity hop,
Up he goes
To the treetop!

Whirly, twirly,
Round and round,
Down he scampers
To the ground.

Furly, curly,
What a tail!
Tall as a feather,
Broad as a sail!

Where's his supper?
In the shell,
Snap, cracky,
Out it fell.

WHITE SHEEP

White sheep, white sheep
On a blue hill.
When the wind stops
You all stand still.
When the wind blows
You walk away slow.
White sheep, white sheep,
Where do you go?

Christina Rossetti

FISHY, FISHY

Fishy, Fishy,
Come bite my hook;
I'll go captain
And you'll go cook.

HENRY

Henry, he is a good
   fisherman,
Catches hens, puts them
   in a pen,
Some lay eggs, some lay
   none.
Wiar, briar, lumber lock,
Three geese in the flock.

FISHY, FISHY

Fishy, Fishy in the brook,
Papa catch him by the hook,
Mama fry him in the pan,
Georgy eat him fast's can.

THE CROCODILE

How doth the little crocodile
   Improve his shining tail,
And pour the waters of the Nile
   On every golden scale!

How cheerfully he seems to grin!
   How neatly spread his claws,
And welcomes little fishes in
   With gently smiling jaws!

Lewis Carroll

A FISH ALIVE

One, two, three, four, five,
I caught a fish alive.
Six, seven, eight, nine, ten,
I let it go again.
Why did you let it go?
Because it bit my finger so.

THE BARNYARD

Oh, I had a bird and the bird
    pleased me,
And I fed my bird under yonder tree,
And the bird went (whistle)

I had a cat and the cat pleased me,
And I fed my cat under yonder tree,
And the cat went (meow)
And the bird went (whistle)

I had a duck and the duck pleased me,
And I fed my duck under yonder tree,
And the duck went (quack)
And the cat went (meow)
And the bird went (whistle)

I had a dog and the dog pleased me,
I fed my dog under yonder tree,
And the dog went (woof)
And the duck went (quack)
And the cat went (meow)
And the bird went (whistle)

I had a goose and the goose pleased me,
And I fed my goose under yonder tree,
And the goose went (honk)
And the dog went (woof)
And the duck went (quack)
And the cat went (meow)
And the bird went (whistle)

I had a turkey and the turkey
    pleased me,
And I fed my turkey under yonder tree,
And the turkey went (gobble)
And the goose went (honk)
And the dog went (woof)
And the duck went (quack)
And the cat went (meow)
And the bird went (whistle)

A FOX WENT OUT ONE WINTER'S NIGHT

A fox went out one winter's night,
And begged the moon to give him light,
For he'd many miles to trot that night
Before he reached his den O!
    Den O! Den O!

The first place he came to was a farmer's yard,
Where the ducks and the geese declared it hard
That their nerves should be shaken and their rest so marred
By a visit from Mr. Fox O!
    Fox O! Fox O!

He took the gray goose by the sleeve,
Says he, "Madam Goose, by your leave
I'll take you away, I do believe,
And carry you home to my den O!
    Den O! Den O!"

He seized the old duck by his neck
And swung him right across his back;
The old duck cried out, "Quack, quack, quack,"
With his legs hanging dangling down O!
    Down O! Down O!"

Old Mother Slipper Slopper jumped out of bed,
And out of the window she popped her head:
"Oh! John! John! the gray goose is gone,
And the fox is off to his den O!
    Den O! Den O!"

John ran up to the top of the hill,
And blew his whistle loud and shrill,
Said the fox, "That is very pretty music; still—
I'd rather be in my den O!
    Den O! Den O!"

The fox went back to his hungry den,
And his dear little foxes, eight, nine, ten;
Quoth they, "Good Daddy, you must go there again,
If you bring such good cheer from the farm O!
    Farm O! Farm O!"

The fox and his wife, without any strife,
(They did very well without fork or knife),
They never ate better duck in their life,
And the little ones picked the bones O!
    Bones O! Bones O!

61

A VISIT FROM ST. NICHOLAS

'Twas the night before Christmas,
    when all through the house
Not a creature was stirring, not
    even a mouse;
The stockings were hung by the
    chimney with care,
In hopes that St. Nicholas soon
    would be there.
The children were nestled all
    snug in their beds,

While visions of sugar-plums
    danced in their heads;
And mamma in her 'kerchief,
    and I in my cap,
Had just settled our brains for a
    long winter's nap,
When out on the lawn there
    arose such a clatter,
I sprang from my bed to see what
    was the matter.

Away to the window I flew like a
	flash,
Tore open the shutters and
	threw up the sash.
The moon on the breast of the
	new-fallen snow
Gave the luster of midday to
	objects below,
When, what to my wondering
	eyes should appear,
But a miniature sleigh, and eight
	tiny reindeer,
With a little old driver, so lively
	and quick,
I knew in a moment it must be
	St. Nick.
More rapid than eagles his
	coursers they came,
And he whistled, and shouted,
	and called them by name:
"Now, Dasher! now, Dancer!
	now, Prancer and Vixen!
On, Comet! on, Cupid! on,
	Donder and Blitzen!
To the top of the porch! to the
	top of the wall!
Now dash away! dash away! dash
	away all!"
As dry leaves that before the wild
	hurricane fly,
When they meet with an
	obstacle, mount to the sky,

So up to the housetop the
	coursers they flew,
With the sleigh full of toys, and
	St. Nicholas, too.
And then, in a twinkling, I heard
	on the roof
The prancing and pawing of each
	little hoof.
As I drew in my head, and was
	turning around,
Down the chimney St. Nicholas
	came with a bound.
He was dressed all in fur, from his
	head to his foot,
And his clothes were all covered
	with ashes and soot;
A bundle of toys he had flung on
	his back,
And he looked like a peddler just
	opening his pack.
His eyes—how they twinkled! his
	dimples how merry!
His cheeks were like roses, his
	nose like a cherry!
His droll little mouth was drawn
	up like a bow,
And the beard on his chin was as
	white as the snow;

The stump of a pipe he held tight
    in his teeth,
And the smoke it encircled his
    head like a wreath;
He had a broad face and a little
    round belly
That shook, when he laughed,
    like a bowlful of jelly.
He was chubby and plump, a
    right jolly old elf,
And I laughed when I saw him,
    in spite of myself;
A wink of his eye and a twist of
    his head,
Soon gave me to know I had
    nothing to dread;

He spoke not a word, but went
    straight to his work,
And filled all the stockings; then
    turned with a jerk,
And laying his finger aside of his
    nose
And giving a nod, up the
    chimney he rose;
He sprang to his sleigh, to his
    team gave a whistle,
And away they all flew like the
    down of a thistle.
But I heard him exclaim, ere he
    drove out of sight,
"Merry Christmas to all, and to
    all a good night."

Clement Clarke Moore

64

A SLEDDING SONG

Sing a song of winter,
    Of frosty clouds in air!
Sing a song of snowflakes
    Falling everywhere.

Sing a song of winter!
    Sing a song of sleds!
Sing a song of tumbling
    Over heels and heads.

Up and down the hillside
    When the moon is bright,
Sledding is a tiptop
    Wintertime delight.

Norman C. Schlichter

DAY BEFORE CHRISTMAS

We have been helping with the cake
    And licking out the pan,
And wrapping up our packages
    As neatly as we can.
And we have hung our stockings up
    Beside the open grate.
Now there's nothing more to do
    Except
        to
           wait!

Marchette Chute

SANTA IS COMING

Oh, clap your hands
And sing with glee!
For Christmas is coming
And merry are we.

How swift o'er the snow
The tiny reindeer
Are flying and bringing
Good Santa Claus near.

Our stocking we'll hang
And while we're asleep,
Down though the chimney
Will Santa Claus creep.

He'll empty his sack
And quickly go back,
Then he'll climb in his sleigh
And hurry away.

So clap, clap your hands
And sing out with glee,
For Christmas is coming
And merry are we.

RAIN ON THE GREEN GRASS

Rain on the green grass,
  Rain on the tree,
Rain on the house-top,
  But don't rain on me.

YOU LOOK

You look, you look, you look,
Like you stole your mother's
    pocketbook.
You took a dime and bought
    some wine
And now you look like
    Frankenstein.

SKIP TO MY LOU

Skip, skip, skip to my Lou,
Skip to my Lou, my darling.

Lost my partner, what'll I do?
Lost my partner, what'll I do?

Skip to my Lou, my darling.
Skip to my Lou, my darling.

I'll find another one prettier than you,
I'll find another one prettier than you,

Skip to my Lou, my darling.
Skip to my Lou, my darling.

Flies in the buttermilk, shoo, fly, shoo,
Flies in the buttermilk, shoo, fly, shoo,

Skip to my Lou, my darling.
Skip to my Lou, my darling.

Red wagon painted blue,
Red wagon painted blue,

Skip to my Lou, my darling.
Skip to my Lou, my darling.

Had one dollar, wish I had two,
Had one dollar, wish I had two,

Skip to my Lou, my darling.
Skip to my Lou, my darling.

THERE WAS A LITTLE WOMAN

There was a little woman
    As I have heard tell,
She went to market
    Her eggs for to sell;
She went to market
    All on a market day,
And she fell asleep
    On the king's highway.
There came by a peddler,
    His name was Stout,
He cut her petticoats
    All round about;
He cut her petticoats
    Up to her knees;
Which made the little woman
    To shiver and sneeze.
When this little woman
    Began to awake,
She began to shiver,
    And she began to shake;
She began to shake,
    And she began to cry,
Lawk a mercy on me,
    This is none of I!

But if this be I,
    and I do hope it do be,
I have a little dog at home
    And he knows me;
If it be I,
    He'll wag his little tail,
And if it be not I
    He'll loudly bark and wail!

Home went the little woman
    All in the dark,
Up starts the little dog,
    And he began to bark;
He began to bark;
    And she began to cry,
Lawk a mercy on me,
    This is none of I!

THE MAD OLD WOMAN

There was an old woman
    And nothing she had.
And this old woman
    Was said to be mad.
She'd nothing to eat,
    And nothing to wear,
She'd nothing to lose,
    And nothing to fear.
She'd nothing to ask,
    And nothing to give,
And when she died,
    She'd nothing to leave.

FELICIA ROPPS

Funny, how Felicia Ropps
Always handles things in shops!
Always pinching, always poking,
Always feeling, always stroking
Things she has no right to touch!
Goops like that annoy me much!

"FIRE, FIRE!" SAID MRS. McGUIRE

"Fire, fire!" said Mrs. McGuire.
"Where, where?" said Mrs. Ware.
"Downtown!" said Mrs. Brown.
"Heaven save us!" said Mrs. Davis.

I WENT DOWNTOWN

I went downtown
To see Mrs. Brown.
She gave me a nickel
To buy a pickle.
The pickle was sour,
She gave me a flower.
The flower was dead,
She gave me a thread.
The thread was thin,
She gave me a pin.
The pin was sharp,
She gave me a harp.
The harp began to sing,
Minnie and a Minnie
    and a ha ha ha.

COBBLER, COBBLER

Cobbler, cobbler, mend my shoe.
Get it done by half past two.

OH SAY

Oh say, kid!
What do you think I did?
I upset the go-cart
And out fell the kid.
The kid began to holler—
I grabbed him by the collar.
The collar broke loose,
And I got the deuce.

HOLDING HANDS

Elephants walking
Along the trails

Are holding hands
By holding tails.

Trunks and tails
Are handy things

When elephants walk
In circus rings.

Elephants work
And elephants play

And elephants walk
And feel so gay.

And when they walk—
It never fails

They're holding hands
By holding tails.

Lenore M. Link

ELETELEPHONY

Once there was an elephant,
Who tried to use the telephant—
No! no! I mean an elephone
Who tried to use the telephone—
(Dear me! I am not certain quite
That even now I've got it right.)

Howe'er it was, he got his trunk
Entangled in the telephunk;
The more he tried to get it free,
The louder buzzed the telephee—
(I fear I'd better drop the song
Of elephop and telephong!)

Laura E. Richards

A GRASSHOPPER STEPPED ON AN ELEPHANT'S TOE

A grasshopper stepped on an
     elephant's toe.
The elephant said, with tears in
     his eyes,
"Pick on somebody your own size."

THE ELEPHANT CARRIES A GREAT BIG TRUNK

The elephant carries a great big
     trunk.
He never packs it with clothes;
It has no lock and it has no key,
But he takes it wherever he goes.

70

LAUGHING TIME

It was laughing time, and the tall Giraffe
Lifted his head and began to laugh:
Ha! Ha! Ha! Ha!

And the Chimpanzee on the ginkgo tree
Swung merrily down with a Tee Hee Hee:
Hee! Hee! Hee! Hee!

"It's certainly not against the law!"
Croaked Justice Crow with a loud guffaw:
Haw! Haw! Haw! Haw!

The dancing Bear who could never say
"No!"
Ho! Ho! Ho! Ho!

The Donkey daintily took his paw,
And around they went:
Hee-Haw! Hee-Haw!
Hee-Haw! Hee-Haw!

The Moon had to smile as it started to climb;
All over the world it was laughing time!
Ho! Ho! Ho! Ho! Hee-Haw! Hee-Haw!
Hee! Hee! Hee! Hee! Ha! Ha! Ha! Ha!

UNCLE JOHN

Uncle John is sick in bed.
    What shall we send him?
Three good wishes,
Three good kisses,
    And a slice of gingerbread.
Who shall we send it by?
    By the fireman's daughter.
Take her by her pretty hand,
    And lead her across the water.

NICHOLAS NED

Nicholas Ned,
    He lost his head,
And put on a turnip instead;
    But then, ah, me!
    He could not see,
So he thought it was night,
    And went to bed.

Laura E. Richards

JEMMY JED

Jemmy Jed went into a shed,
And made a ted of straw his bed;
An owl came out, and flew about,
And Jemmy up stakes and fled.
Wasn't Jemmy Jed a staring fool,
Born in the woods to be scared
    by an owl?

LITTLE DICK

Little Dick,
He was so quick,
He tumbled over a timber,
He bent his bow,
To shoot a crow,
And shot the cat in the winder.

IT HAPPEN'D UPON A CERTAIN DAY

It happen'd upon a certain day,
A lady went to church to pray.

When she came to the church stile,
There she did rest a little while;
When she came to the churchyard,
There the bells so loud she heard.

When she came to the church door,
She stopped to rest a little more;
When she came to the church within,
The parson pray'd gainst pride and sin.

On looking up, on looking down,
She saw a dead man on the ground;
And from his nose unto his chin,
The worms crawl'd out,
    the worms crawl'd in.

Then she unto the parson said,
Shall I be so when I am dead:
"O yes! O yes!" The parson said,
You will be so when you are dead.

OLD FRED

Here lies old Fred.
It's a pity he is dead.
We would rather
It had been his father;
Had it been his sister,
We would have not missed her;
If the whole generation,
So much the better for the nation,
But since it is only Fred
Who was alive, and is now dead,
There is no more to be said.

WYNKEN, BLYNKEN, AND NOD

Wynken, Blynken, and Nod one night
    Sailed off in a wooden shoe,
Sailed on a river of crystal light,
    Into a sea of dew.
"Where are you going, and what do you wish?"
    The old moon asked the three.
"We have come to fish for the herring fish
    That live in this beautiful sea;
    Nets of silver and gold have we!"
        Said Wynken,
        Blynken,
        and Nod.

The old moon laughed and sang a song,
    As they rocked in the wooden shoe;
And the wind that sped them all night long
    Ruffled the waves of dew.
The little stars were the herring fish
    That lived in that beautiful sea—
"Now cast your nets wherever you wish—
    But never afeared are we";
    So cried the stars to the fishermen three:
        Wynken,
        Blynken,
        and Nod.

NEW MOON

New moon, true moon,
Star in the stream,
Pray tell my fortune
In my dream.

All night long their nets they threw
    To the stars in the twinkling foam,
Then down from the skies came the wooden shoe,
    Bringing the fishermen home;
'Twas all so pretty a sail, it seemed
    As if it could not be;
And some folk thought 'twas a dream they'd dreamed
    Of sailing that beautiful sea—
    But I shall name you the fishermen three:
        Wynken,
        Blynken,
        and Nod.

Wynken and Blynken are two little eyes,
    And Nod is a little head,
And the wooden shoe that sailed the skies
    Is a wee one's trundle-bed.
So shut your eyes while Mother sings
    Of wonderful sights that be,
And you shall see the beautiful things
    As you rock in the misty sea,
    Where the old shoe rocked the fishermen three:
        Wynken,
        Blynken,
        and Nod.

Eugene Field

THE MONTHS

January brings the snow,
Makes our feet and fingers glow.

February brings the rain,
Thaws the frozen lake again.

March brings breezes loud and shrill,
Stirs the dancing daffodil.

April brings the primrose sweet,
Scatters daisies at our feet.

May brings flocks of pretty lambs,
Skipping by their fleecy dams.

June brings tulips, lilies, roses,
Fills the children's hands with posies.

Hot July brings cooling showers,
Apricots and gillyflowers.

August brings the sheaves of corn,
Then the harvest home is borne.

Warm September brings the fruit,
Sportsmen then begin to shoot.

Fresh October brings the pheasant,
Then to gather nuts is pleasant.

Dull November brings the blast,
Then the leaves are whirling fast.

Chill December brings the sleet,
Blazing fire, and Christmas treat.

Sara Coleridge

TIME TO RISE

A birdie with a yellow bill
Hopped upon my window sill,
Cocked his shining eye and said:
"Time to rise, you sleepy head!"

Robert Lewis Stevenson

SPIDER'S INVITATION

Early in the morn the spiders spin,
And by and by the flies drop in;
And when they call, the spiders say
"Take off your things, and stay all day."

MONDAY MORNING

I woke up Monday morning
    And gazed upon the wall.
The spiders and the fireflies were
    Playing a game of ball.

The score was ten to twelve,
    The spiders were ahead,
The fireflies knocked a home run
    And knocked me out of bed!

I went down to breakfast,
    The bread was hard and stale,
The coffee tasted like tobacco juice
    Right out of County Jail.

Emma Victor Worstell

A LITTLE BIRD

I saw a little bird, come
        hop, hop, hop.
So I said, "Little bird, will you
        Stop, stop, stop?"
I went to the window to say,
        "How do you do?"
But he shook his little tail,
        And away he flew.

PIGEONS AND CROWS

Pigeons and crows,
Take care of your toes,
Or I'll pick up my crackers
and knock you over backwards.

THE THREE LITTLE KITTENS

Three little kittens lost their mittens,
And they began to cry,
"Oh, Mother dear,
We sadly fear
Our mittens we have lost."
"Lost your mittens!
You naughty kittens!
Then you shall have no pie!"
"Mee-ow, mee-ow, mee-ow."
"No, you shall have no pie!"
"Mee-ow, mee-ow, mee-ow."

The three little kittens found their mittens
And they began to cry,
"Oh, Mother dear,
See here, see here!
See, we have found our mittens!"
"Put on your mittens,
You silly kittens,
And you may have some pie."
"Purr-r, purr-r, purr-r,
Oh, let us have the pie!
Purr-r, purr-r, purr-r."

The three little kittens put on their mittens,
And soon ate up the pie;
"Oh, Mother dear,
We greatly fear
That we have soiled our mittens!"
"Soiled your mittens!
You naughty kittens!"
Then they began to sigh,
"Mee-ow, mee-ow, mee-ow."
Then they began to sigh,
"Mee-ow, mee-ow, mee-ow."

The three little kittens washed their mittens,
And hung them out to dry;
"Oh, Mother dear,
Do not you hear
That we have washed our mittens?"
"What? Washed your mittens!
Oh, what good kittens!
But I smell a rat close by,
Hush, hush! Mee-ow, mee-ow,"
"We smell a rat close,
Mee-ow, mee-ow, mee-ow."

Liza Lee Follen

79

NOT LAST NIGHT

Not last night
        but the night before
Twenty-four robbers
        came knocking on my door,
And this is what they said:
"Buster, Buster, hands on head;
Buster, Buster, go to bed;
Buster, Buster, if you don't,
I'm afraid they'll find you dead."

SOMEONE

Someone came knocking
At my wee small door;
Someone came knocking,
I'm sure—sure—sure;
I listened, I opened,
I looked to left and right,
But nought there was a-stirring
In the still dark night.
Only the busy beetle
Tap-tapping in the wall,
Only from the forest
The screech-owl's call,
Only the cricket whistling
While the dew drops fall,
So I know not who came knocking,
At all, at all, at all.

Walter de la Mare

AS I WAS GOING UP THE STAIR

As I was going up the stair
I met a man who wasn't there.
He wasn't there again today—
Oh, how I wish he'd go away!

80

CHARLIE CHAPLIN

Charlie Chaplin went to France
To teach the ladies how to dance.
Heel, toe, and around we go;
Salute to the captain,
Bow to the queen,
Turn your back
On the old submarine.

THE GRAND OLD DUKE OF YORK

The Grand Old Duke of York,
He had ten thousand men.
He marched them up to the top of the hill,
And he marched them down again.

And when they were up, they were up,
And when they were down they were down,
And when they were only half way up
They were neither up nor down.

YANKEE DOODLE

Yankee Doodle went to town,
Upon a little pony;
He stuck a feather in his cap,
And called it Macaroni.

Yankee Doodle went to town,
He bought a bag of peaches,
He rode so fast a-coming back,
He smashed them all to pieces.

Yankee Doodle, keep it up,
Yankee Doodle dandy!
Mind the music and the steps,
And with the girls be handy.

SAILOR OVER THE SEA

Sailor, sailor, over the sea,
Give me a cup of tea.
If you have none,
Give me a bun.
Sailor, sailor, over the sea.

JOHNNY OVER THE OCEAN

Johnny over the ocean,
Johnny over the sea,
Johnny broke a teacup
And blamed it all on me.

SALLY OVER THE WATER

Sally over the water,
Sally over the sea,
Sally broke a milk bottle
And blamed it on me.
Sally told Ma,
Ma told Pa,
Sally got a scolding,
Ha, ha, ha.

A SAILOR WENT TO SEA

A sailor went to sea
To see what he could see,
And all that he could see,
Was the sea, sea, sea.

THE BOY STOOD ON THE BURNING DECK

The boy stood on the burning deck,
Eating peanuts by the peck.
A girl stood by all dressed in blue,
And said, "I guess I'll have some too."

The boy stood on the burning deck,
His feet were full of blisters.
The flames came up and burned his
    pants,
Now he wears his sister's.

IF ALL THE SEAS WERE ONE SEA

If all the seas were one sea,
What a great sea that would be!
If all the trees were one tree,
What a great tree that would be!
If all the axes were one axe,
What a great axe that would be!
If all the men were one man,
What a great man that would be!
And if the great man took the great
    axe,
And cut down the great tree,
And let it fall into the great sea,
What a splish-splash that would be!

DONKEY, DONKEY

Donkey, donkey, old and gray,
Open your mouth and gently bray.
Lift your ears and blow your horn
To wake the world this sleepy morn.

I HAD A LITTLE COLT

I had a little colt,
His name was Jack;
I put him in the barn,
But he jumped through the crack.

BUZZ, BUZZ, BUZZ

A bumblebee flew over the barn,
A great big bundle under his arm.
What you don't know won't do you no harm.
Buzz, buzz, buzz.

OLD HOGAN'S GOAT

Old Hogan's goat
Was feeling fine.
He ate a red shirt
Right off my line.
I took a stick
And beat his back
And tied him to
A railroad track.
A speeding train
Was adrawin' nigh;
Old Hogan's goat
Was doomed to die.
He gave an awful
Shriek of pain,
Coughed up that shirt
And flagged that train.

CHICK, CHICK

Chick, chick, chatterman,
How much are your geese?
Chick, chick, chatterman,
Five cents apiece.
Chick, chick, chatterman,
That's too dear.
Chick, chick, chatterman,
Get out of here.

THERE WAS A LITTLE PIG

There was a little pig,
  Who didn't grow big,
    So they put him in a great big show.
He tumbled through a winder
  And broke his little finger.
    Now he can't play his old banjo.

HIPPITY HOP

Hippity hop to the barber shop
To buy a stick of candy;
One for me and one for you,
And one for sister Mandy.

GO TELL AUNT RHODY

Go tell Aunt Rhody
The old gray goose is dead,
The one that she was saving,
To make a feather bed.
The old gander is a-mourning,
Because his wife is dead,
The little goslings weeping,
Because their mammy's dead.
The whole family's weeping,
Because the gray goose is dead.

A RABBIT SKIPPED

A rabbit skipped
A rabbit hopped
A rabbit ate
A turnip top.

I WENT DOWN TO GRANDPA'S FARM

I went down to Grandpa's farm,
A billy goat chased me round the barn,
He chased me up the sycamore tree,
And this is the song he sang to me:
"I love coffee, I love tea,
I love the boys and the boys love me."

SHOE THE OLD HORSE

Shoe the old horse, shoe the old mare,
Drive a nail here, and drive a nail there;
But let the little nobby colt go bare.

85

THIS OLD MAN

This old man he played one,
He played tick tack on his thumb.
Nick nack, paddy whack, give a dog a bone,
This old man came rolling home.

This old man he played two,
He played tick tack on his shoe.
Nick nack, paddy whack, give a dog a bone,
This old man came rolling home.

This old man he played three,
He played tick tack on his knee.
Nick nack, paddy whack, give a dog a bone,
This old man came rolling home.

This old man he played four,
He played tick tack on a door.
Nick nack, paddy whack, give a dog a bone,
This old man came rolling home.

This old man he played five,
He played tick tack on a hive.
Nick nack, paddy whack, give a dog a bone,
This old man came rolling home.

This old man he played six,
He played tick tack on some sticks.
Nick nack, paddy whack, give a dog a bone,
This old man came rolling home.

This old man he played seven,
He played tick tack up to heaven.
Nick nack, paddy whack, give a dog a bone,
This old man came rolling home.

This old man he played eight,
He played tick tack on a gate.
Nick nack, paddy whack, give a dog a bone,
This old man came rolling home.

This old man he played nine,
He played tick tack on a line.
Nick nack, paddy whack, give a dog a bone,
This old man came rolling home.

This old man he played ten,
He played tick tack on a pen,
Nick nack, paddy whack, give a dog a bone,
This old man came rolling home.

THERE WAS A PIG

There was a pig, that sat alone,
    Beside a ruined pump.
By day and night he made his moan:
It would have stirred a heart of stone
    To see him wring his hoofs and groan,
Because he could not jump.

Lewis Carroll

MONKEY, MONKEY

Monkey, monkey, sitting on a rail,
Picking his teeth with the end of his tail.

TIRED TIM

Poor tired Tim! It's sad for him;
He lags the long bright morning through,
Ever so tired of nothing to do;
He moons and mopes the live long day,
Nothing to think about, nothing to say;
Up to bed with his candle to creep,
Too tired to yawn, too tired to sleep:
Poor tired Tim! It's sad for him.

Walter de la Mare

BEFORE YOU CROSS
THE STREET

Stop! Look! Listen!
Before you cross the street,
Use your eyes;
Use your ears;
Before you use your feet!

UP THE RIVER

Up the river,
Down the lake;
Teacher's got a bellyache.
If she says your work is bad.
Tell her that you are so sad.

TWO'S A COUPLE

Two's a couple,
Three's a crowd,
Four on the sidewalk
Is never allowed.

WAY DOWN SOUTH

Way down South where
    bananas grow,
A grasshopper stepped
    on an elephant's toe.
The elephant said, with
    tears in his eyes,
"Pick on somebody your
    own size."

SPIDERS

If you see a spider at night,
It will bring you joy and delight,
If you see a spider in the morning,
Beware, and take warning.

SPIDERS SPIN

At early morning the spiders spin,
And by and by the flies drop in.
When they call, the spiders say:
Take off your things, and stay all day.

I WENT TO THE ANIMAL FAIR

I went to the animal fair;
The birds and the beasts were there.
The big baboon by the light of the moon
Was combing his auburn hair.

The monkey he got drunk;
And sat on the elephant's trunk.
The elephant sneezed and fell on his knees
And that was the end of the monkey-monk.

A HORSE AND A FLEA

A horse and a flea and three blind mice
Sat on a curbstone shooting dice.
The horse he slipped and fell on the flea.
The flea said, "Oops, there a horse on me!"

THE SAUSAGE

The sausage is a cunning bird
With feathers long and wavy.
It swims in a frying pan
And makes its nest in gravy.

JACK A NORY

I'll tell you a story
About Jack a Nory,
He had a calf,
And that's the half;
He threw it over the wall
And that's all.

THE OWL AND THE PUSSYCAT

The Owl and the Pussycat went to sea
    In a beautiful pea-green boat:
They took some honey, and plenty of money
    Wrapped up in a five-pound note.
The Owl looked up to the stars above,
    And sang to a small guitar,
"O lovely Pussy, O Pussy, my love,
    What a beautiful Pussy you are,
        You are,
        You are,
    What a beautiful Pussy you are!"

Pussy said to the Owl, "You elegant fowl,
    How charmingly sweet you sing!
Oh! let us be married; too long we have tarried:
    But what shall we do for a ring?"
They sailed away, for a year and a day,
    To the land where the bong tree grows;
And there in a wood a Piggy-wig stood,
    With a ring at the end of his nose,
        His nose,
        His nose,
    With a ring at the end of his nose.

"Dear Pig, are you willing to sell for one shilling
    Your ring?" Said the Piggy, "I will."
So they took it away, and were married next day
    By the Turkey who lives on the hill.
They dined on mince and slices of quince,
    Which they ate with a runcible spoon;
And hand in hand, on the edge of the sand,
    They danced by the light of the moon,
        The moon,
        The moon,
    They danced by the light of the moon.

Edward Lear

JOHNNY GAVE ME APPLES

Johnny gave me apples,
Johnny gave me pears,
Johnny gave me fifteen cents,
And kissed me on the stairs.

THE BEE'S MISTAKE

What do you suppose?
A bee sat on my nose.
Then what do you think?
He said, "I beg your pardon,
I thought you were the garden."

FIVE LITTLE PEAS

Five little peas in a peapod pressed,
One grew, two grew, and so did all the rest.
They grew and they grew and they did not stop,
Till all of a sudden the pod went POP!

I WENT UP THE APPLE TREE

As I went up the apple tree,
All the apples fell on me.
Baked in a pudding, baked in a pie,
Did you ever tell a lie?
You know you did, you know you did!
You broke your mother's teapot lid.
She blew you in, she blew you out.
She blew you in the teapot spout.

MISTER BEERS

This is Mister Beers;
    And for forty-seven years
He's been digging in his
garden like a miner.
    He isn't planting seeds
    Nor scratching up weeds,
He's trying to dig a tunnel
down to China.

Hugh Lofting

THE ERIE CANAL

I've got a mule, her name is Sal,
Fifteen years on the Erie Canal.
She's a good old worker and a good old pal,
Fifteen years on the Erie Canal.
We've haul'd some barges in our day,
Fill'd with lumber, coal, and hay,
And we know ev'ry inch of the way
From Albany to Buffalo.

Low bridge, ev'rybody down!
Low bridge, for we're going through a town,
And you'll always know your neighbor,
You'll always know your pal,
If you ever navigated on the Erie Canal.

We better get along on our way, old gal,
Fifteen years on the Erie Canal,
'Cause you bet your life I'd never part with Sal,
Fifteen years on the Erie Canal.

Low bridge, ev'rybody down! *etc*.

Git up there, mule, here comes a lock,
We'll make Rome 'bout six o'clock,
One more trip and back we'll go
Right back home to Buffalo.

Low bridge, ev'rybody down! *etc*.

ALGY

Algy met a bear.
A bear met Algy.
The bear was bulgy.
The bulge was Algy.

FUZZY WUZZY

Fuzzy Wuzzy was a bear.
Fuzzy Wuzzy had no hair.
So Fuzzy Wuzzy wasn't fuzzy,
     was he?

TEDDY BEAR, TEDDY BEAR

Teddy Bear, Teddy Bear,
     Go upstairs.
Teddy Bear, Teddy Bear,
     Say your prayers.
Teddy Bear, Teddy Bear,
     Turn out the light.
Teddy Bear, Teddy Bear,
     Say good night.

OLD JOE CLARK

Old Joe Clark had a house,
     It was sixteen stories high,
And every room in that house
     Smelled of apple pie.

Old Joe Clark had a horse,
     Name was Morgan Brown,
And everywhere that horse went
     He covered an acre of ground.

Old Joe Clark had a dog
     As blind as blind can be.
He chased a possum round a tree,
     I bet that dog could see.

Round and round, old Joe Clark,
     Round and round we've gone.
Bye, bye to you Old Joe Clark
     And bye, bye Lucy Long.

PICNIC

Ella, fella
Maple tree.
Hilda, build a
Fire for me.

Teresa, squeeze a
Lemon, so.
Amanda, handa
Plate to Flo.

Nora, pour a
Cup of tea.
Fancy, Nancy,
What a spree!

Hugh Lofting

LEMONADE

Lemonade,
Made in the shade,
Stirred with a spade
By an old maid.

A BIG BUMBLEBEE

A big bumblebee
Sat on a wall;
He said he could hum
And that was all.

I SCREAM

I scream, you scream,
We all scream for ice cream.

GARDEN PATCH

I went down to my garden patch
To see if my old hen had hatched.
She'd hatched out her chickens and
    the peas were green;
She sat there a-pickin' on a tambourine.

PINK ICE CREAM

When you pass pink ice cream,
Don't act as if you'd like to scream.
Turn your head the other way—
Act like you had it EVERY day.

95

ANNA ELISE

Anna Elise,
She jumped with surprise;
The surprise was so quick,
It played her a trick.
The trick was so rare,
She jumped on a chair;
The chair was so frail,
She jumped in a pail;
The pail was so wet,
She jumped in a net;
The net was so small,
She jumped on a ball;
The ball was so round,
She jumped on the ground;
And ever since then
She's been turning around.

THE PURPLE COW

I never saw a Purple Cow,
    I hope I never see one;
But I can tell you, anyhow,
    I'd rather see than be one.

Gelett Burgess

SPEAK TO ME

Speak to me, darlin',
    Oh, speaky, spikey, spokey.
Why are those tears
    On your cheeky, chikey, chokey?
Give me the answer
    I seeky, sikey, sokey!
Or else I'll go jump
    In the creeky, crikey, crokey.

I HAD AN OLD MULE

I had an old mule
His name was Jack,
I rode on his tail to save his back.
The lightning roll and the thunder flash
And it split my coat-tail
All to smash.

POLICEMAN

Policeman, policeman, don't catch me!
Catch the boy behind the tree.
He took money, I took none;
Put him in the jailhouse, just for fun!

I HAD A COW

I had a cow that gave such milk
I dressed her in the finest silk;
I fed her on the finest hay,
And milked her twenty times a day.

PETER SIMON

Peter Simon Suckegg

Traded his wife for a duck egg.

The duck egg was rotten,

So he traded for cotton.

The cotton was yellow,

So he traded for tallow.

The tallow was soft,

So he traded for a calf.

The calf was too little,

So he traded for a kettle.

The kettle was black,

So he traded for a jack.

The jack wouldn't bray,

So he traded for a sleigh.

The sleigh wouldn't scoot,

So he traded for a boot.

The boot was too big,

So he traded for a pig.

The pig wouldn't squeal,

So he traded for a wheel.

The wheel wouldn't turn,

So he traded for a churn.

The churn wouldn't flicker,

So he traded it for licker.

The licker was stale,

So they put him in jail.

PUSSY

Pussy has a whiskered face,
Kitty has such pretty ways;
Doggie scampers when I call,
And has a heart to love us all.

Christina Rossetti

THE CATS OF KILKENNY

There were once two cats of Kilkenny.
Each thought there was one cat too many.
So they fought and they fit,
And they scratched and they bit,
Till excepting their nails,
And the tips of their tails,
Instead of two cats there weren't any.

I LOVE LITTLE PUSSY

I love little Pussy.
Her coat is so warm,
And if I don't hurt her,
She'll do me no harm.
So I'll not pull her tail,
Or drive her away,
But Pussy and I
Very gently will play.
She will sit by my side,
And I'll give her her food,
And she'll like me because
I am gentle and good.

I'll pat little Pussy,
And then she will purr,
And thus show her thanks
For my kindness to her;
I'll not pinch her ears,
Nor tread on her paws,
Lest I should provoke her
To use her sharp claws;
I never will vex her,
Nor make her displeased,
For Pussy can't bear
To be worried or teased.

Jane Taylor

MOTHER CAT

There was a mother cat,
Who ate a ball of yarn,
And when she had kittens,
They all had sweaters on.

THE MOUSE WHO LIVED ON A HILL

There once was a mouse who lived on
    a hill;
    uh-huh...uh-huh
He huffed and puffed like Buffalo Bill.
    uh-huh...uh-huh
One day he thought he'd go for a ride,
With his sword and pistol by his side.
    uh-huh...uh-huh
He rode up to Miss Mousie's door,
And knocked and knocked 'til his fist
    got sore.
    uh-huh...uh-huh
He sat Miss Mousie on his knee,
    uh-huh...uh-huh
And said, "Please, Miss Mouse, will
    you marry me?"
    uh-huh...uh-huh
Miss Mousie replied, "I can't do that;

I'll have to ask my brother rat."
    uh-huh...uh-huh
Her brother rat was gone to town,
    uh-huh...uh-huh
To buy Miss Mousie a wedding gown.
    uh-huh...uh-huh
The wedding was held in an old oak
    tree,
    uh-huh...uh-huh
With cornbread, cabbage, and black-
    eye peas.
    uh-huh...uh-huh
They had four children that looked
    like rats,
    uh-huh...uh-huh
All tall, skinny, short, and fat.
    uh-huh...uh-huh,
    uh-huh...uh-huh

THE SNAIL

The snail lives in his hard round house,
    In the orchard, under the tree:
Says he: "I've but a single room;
    But it's large enough for me."

The snail in his little house doth dwell
    All week from end to end,
You're at home, Master Snail; that's all very well.
    But you never receive a friend.

A CENTIPEDE

A centipede was happy quite,
    Until a frog in fun
Said, "Pray, which leg comes after which?"
This raised her mind to such a pitch,
She lay distracted in the ditch
    Considering how to run.

SNAKE, SNAKE

Snake, snake, run in the grass
And I'll not hurt you as you pass.

THE FROG

What a wonderful bird the frog are—
When he stand he sit almost;
When he hop, he fly almost.
He ain't got no sense hardly;
He ain't got no tail hardly either.
When he sit, he sit on what he ain't got almost.

DON'T EVER CROSS A CROCODILE

Don't ever cross a crocodile,
However few his faults.
Don't ever dare
A dancing bear
To teach you how to waltz.

Don't ever poke a rattlesnake
Who's sleeping in the sun
And say the poke
Was just a joke
And really all in fun.

Don't ever lure a lion close
With gifts of steak and suet.
Though lion-looks
Are nice in books,
Don't ever, ever do it.

Kaye Starbird

IN THE MAPLE SWAMP

Way down yonder in
    the maple swamp
The wild geese gather and
    the ganders honk.
The mare kick up and
    the ponies prance;
The old sow whistles and
    the little pigs prance.

OVER IN THE MEADOW

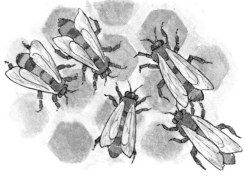

Over in the meadow in the sand in the sun
Lived an old mother turtle and her little turtle one.
Dig said the mother. We dig said the one.
So they dug all day in the sand in the sun.

Over in the meadow where the stream runs blue
Lived an old mother fish and her little fishes two.
Swim said the mother. We swim said the two.
So they swam all day where the stream runs blue.

Over in the meadow in a hole in a tree
Lived an old mother owl and her little owls three.
Tu-whoo said the mother. Tu-whoo said the three.
So they tu-whooed all day in a hole in a tree.

Over in the meadow by the old barn door
Lived an old mother rat and her little ratties four.
Gnaw said the mother. We gnaw said the four.
So they gnawed all day by the old barn door.

Over in the meadow in a snug beehive
Lived an old mother bee and her little bees five.
Buzz said the mother. We buzz said the five.
So they buzzed all day in a snug beehive.

Over in the meadow in a nest built of sticks
Lived an old mother crow and her little crows six.
Caw said the mother. We caw said the six.
So they cawed all day in a nest built of sticks.

Over in the meadow where the grass grows so even
Lived an old mother frog and her little froggies seven.
Jump said the mother. We jump said the seven.
So they jumped all day where the grass grows so even.

Over in the meadow by the old mossy gate
Lived an old mother lizard and her little lizards eight.
Bask said the mother. We bask said the eight.
So they basked all day by the old mossy gate.

Over in the meadow by the old scotch pine
Lived an old mother duck and her little ducks nine.
Quack said the mother. We quack said the nine.
So they quacked all day by the old scotch pine.

Over in the meadow in a cozy wee den
Lived an old mother beaver and her little beavers ten.
Beave said the mother. We beave said the ten.
So they beaved all day in a cozy wee den.

PATIENCE IS A VIRTUE

Patience is a virtue,
Virtue is a grace,
Grace is a little girl
Who wouldn't
Wash her face.

DARLING CHILD

I was my mother's darling child,
Brought up with care and trouble.
For fear a spoon would hurt my mouth,
She fed me with a shovel.

HUCKLEBERRY, GOOSEBERRY, RASPBERRY PIE

Huckleberry, gooseberry, raspberry pie,
All sweetest things one cannot buy.
Peppermint candies are six for a penny,
But true love & kisses, one cannot buy any.

Clyde Watson

MINGLE-DEE, PINGLE-DEE

Mingle-dee, pingle-dee,
   clap-clap-clap—
How many fingers do I hold
   in my lap?
Would you say one?
Would you say two?
Raspberries, strawberries,
Fresh with the dew.
Would you say three?
Would you say four?
Rutabaga, pumpkins,
Onions and corn.
Would you say five?
Would you say six?
Dandelions, crocuses,
Chicory sticks.
Would you say seven?
Would you say eight?
Eggs and cheese muffins
On a dinner plate.
Would you say nine?
Would you say ten?
Then open your eyes
And count them all again.
Mingle-dee, pingle-dee,
   clap-clap-clap—
How many fingers do I hold
   in my lap?

MY BOYFRIEND'S NAME IS JELL-O

My boyfriend's name is Jell-O;
He comes from Monticello,
With a pimple on his nose
And two flat toes.
And that's the way my story goes.

POLLY, DOLLY, KATE AND MOLLY

Polly, Dolly, Kate and Molly,
All are filled with pride and folly.
    Polly tattles,
    Dolly wriggles,
    Katy rattles,
    Molly giggles;
Whoe'er knew such constant rattling,
Wriggling, giggling, noise, and tattling?

DOWN BY THE BAY

Down by the bay
Where the watermelons grow
Back to my home
I dare not go
For if I do
My mother will say
Did you ever see a bee
With a sun-burned knee
Down by the bay?

EEPER WEEPER

Eeper weeper, chimney sweeper,
Had a wife and couldn't keep her,
Had another, didn't love her,
Up the chimney he did shove her.

LITTLE SALLY WATER

Little Sally Water,
Sitting in a saucer;
Rise, Sally, rise,
Wipe off your eyes.
Put your hand on your hip;
Don't let your backbone slip.
Turn to the East, Sally,
Turn to the West,
Turn to the one, Sally,
That you love the best.

EGGS, CHEESE, BUTTER

Eggs, cheese, butter, bread,
Stick, stack, stone dead.
Stick 'em up, stick 'em down,
Stick 'em in the old man's crown.

HINTY, MINTY, CUTY CORN

Hinty, minty, cuty corn,
Apple seed, and apple thorn,
Wire, briar, limber-lock,
Three geese in a flock;
One flew east, one flew west,
One flew over the cuckoo's nest.

LITTLE SISTER HONEY

I had a little sister
And her name was Honey.
She played in the stream
Where the frogs croaked funny.
She ran through the field
With a song on her tongue.
She picked a few flowers
Just for fun.

HIGGLETY, PIGGLETY, POP

Higglety, pigglety, pop!
The dog has eaten the mop;
    The pig's in a hurry,
    The cat's in a flurry,
Higglety, pigglety pop!

SKIPPING

The high skip,
The sly skip,
The skip like a feather.
The long skip,
The strong skip,
The skip all together.
The slow skip,
The toe skip,
The skip double-double.
The fast skip,
The last skip,
The skip against trouble!

Eleanor Farjeon

EENIE, MEENIE, MINIE, MO

Eenie, meenie, minie, mo,
Catch a tiger by the toe,

If he hollers let him go,
Eenie, meenie, minie, mo.

Eenie, meenie, minie, mo,
Catch a thief by the toe,

If he hollers make him pay
Fifty dollars every day.

EENA MEENA DIXIE DAN

Eena meena Dixie Dan,
Who will be a soldier man?
Ride a horse, beat a drum,
Tell me when your birthday comes.

FURRY ONES

I like
the furry ones—
the waggy ones
the purry ones
the hoppy ones
that hurry.

The glossy ones
the saucy ones
the sleepy ones
the leapy ones
the mousy ones
that scurry.

The snuggly ones
the huggly ones
the never, never
ugly ones...
all soft
and warm
and furry.

Aileen Fisher

POEM TO MUD

Poem to mud —
Poem to ooze —
Patted in pies, or coating the shoes,
Poem to slooze—
Poem to crud—
Fed by a leak, or spread by a flood.
Wherever, whenever, whyever it goes,
Stirred by your finger, or strained by your toes,
There's nothing sloopier, slippier, floppier,
There's nothing slickier, stickier, thickier,
There's nothing quickier to make grown-ups
    sickier,
Trulier, coolier,
Than wonderful mud.

Zilpha Keatley Snyder

NOTICE

I have a dog,
I have a cat.
I've got a frog
Inside my hat.

David McCord

DUCK'S DITTY

All along the backwater,
Through the rushes tall,
Ducks are a-dabbling,
Up tails all!
Ducks' tails, drakes' tails,
Yellow feet a-quiver,
Yellow bills all out of sight
Busy in the river!

Slushy green undergrowth
Where the roach swim—
Here we keep our larder,
Cool and full and dim.

Everyone for what he likes!
We like to be
Heads down, tails up,
Dabbling free!

High in the blue above
Swifts whirl and call—
We are down a-dabbling
Up tails all!

Kenneth Grahame

A DUCK, A DRAKE

A duck, a drake, a barley cake,
A penny to pay the baker;
A hop, a scotch, another notch—
Slithery, slithery take her.

DUCKS

Ducks are lucky,
Don't you think?
When they want to
Take a drink,
All they do is
Duck their bill
(Doesn't matter
If they spill).
When they want to
Take a swim,
All they do is
Dive right in;
And they never
Seem to sink.
Ducks are lucky,
Don't you think?

Mary Ann Hoberman

HERE'S A PATIENT

One, two, three a nation,
Come on, Doctor, here's a patient
Waiting for an operation.
One, two, three a nation.

RIN TIN TIN

Rin Tin Tin
Swallowed a pin.
Went to the doctor,
The doctor wasn't in.
He opened the door
And fell on the floor
And that was the end
Of Rin Tin Tin.

MARGUERITE

Marguerite, go wash your feet;
The board of health is 'cross the street.

WHO ARE YOU?

Who are you?
A dirty old man!
I've always been since the day I began.
Mother and Father were dirty before me,
Hot and cold water have never been
     o'er me.

DICKY DAN

Dicky Dan was a funny wee man,
He washed his head in a frying pan,
He combed his hair with the leg
     of a chair,
Dicky Dan was a funny wee man.

OBADIAH

Obadiah jumped in the fire;
The fire was hot, so he jumped in a pot;
The pot was little, so he jumped in the kettle;
The kettle was black, so he jumped in a crack;
The crack was high, so he jumped in the sky;
The sky was blue, so he jumped in a canoe;
The canoe was deep, so he jumped in the creek;
The creek was shallow, so he jumped in the tallow;
The tallow was hard, so he jumped in the lard,
The lard was soft, so he jumped in the loft;
The loft was rotten, so he jumped in the cotton;
The cotton was white, so he stayed all night.

FATTY, FATTY

Fatty, Fatty, two by four,
Hanging around the kitchen door,
When the door begins to shake,
Fatty has a bellyache.

GET UP

Get up, get up, you lazy head.
Get up you lazy sinner.
We need those sheets for tablecloths,
It's nearly time for dinner.

111

COWS LOVE PUMPKINS

Cows love pumpkins,
Pigs love squash,
I love you, I do, by gosh.

THE LITTLE TURTLE

There was a little turtle.
He lived in a box.
He swam in a puddle.
He climbed on the rocks.

He snapped at a mosquito.
He snapped at a flea.
He snapped at a minnow.
And he snapped at me.

He caught the mosquito.
He caught the flea.
He caught the minnow.
But he didn't catch me.

Vachel Lindsay

WHAT?

What is moister than an oyster?
What is slicker than an eel?
What is flatter than a platter?
What is rounder than a wheel?

LITTLE BOY

Little boy, little boy,
Where did you get those britches?
"Father cut them out
And mother sewed the stitches."

Little boy, little boy,
What 'came of your britches?
"Caught them on a nail
And tore out all the stitches."

I WONDER WHY

A pin has a head, but has no hair;
A clock has a face, but no mouth there;
Needles have eyes, but they cannot see;
A fly has a trunk without lock or key;
A timepiece may lose, but cannot win;
A cornfield dimples without a chin;
A hill has no leg, but has a foot;
A wine-glass a stem, but not a root;
Rivers run, though they have no feet;
A saw has teeth, but it does not eat;
Ash-trees have keys, yet never lock;
And a baby crows, without being a cock.

Christina Rossetti

TRAINS

Over the mountains,
Over the plains,
Over the rivers,
Here come the trains.

Carrying passengers,
Carrying mail,
Bringing their precious loads
In without fail.

Thousands of freight cars,
All rushing on
Through day and darkness
Through dusk and dawn.

Over the mountains,
Over the plains,
Over the river,
Here come the trains.

James S. Tippett

ENGINE NUMBER NINE

Engine, engine, number nine,
Sliding down Chicago line;
When she's polished she will shine,
Engine, engine, number nine.

EARLY IN THE MORNING

Let's go to the country.
See the little puff-puffs, all in a row.
Man in the engine pulls a little lever;
Choo-choo, whoo-whoo, off we go.

PEANUT ON THE RAILROAD

A peanut sat on the railroad track,
    His heart was all a-flutter;
Along came a train—the 9:15—
    Toot, toot, peanut butter!

A MODERN DRAGON

A train is a dragon that roars through
    the dark.
He wriggles his tail as sends up a spark.
He pierces the night with his one
    yellow eye,
And all the earth trembles when he
    rushes by.

Rowena Bennett

113

LIAR, LIAR

Liar, liar,
Your tongue shall split,
And all the doggies in the town,
Shall have a tiny bit!

I'M THE LITTLE PUPPY DOG

My father owns the butcher shop
My mother cuts the meat,
And I'm the little puppy dog
That runs down the street.

THERE WAS A NAUGHTY BOY

There was a naughty boy,
And a naughty boy was he,
He ran away to Scotland
   The people for to see—
   There he found
   That the ground
Was as hard,
That a yard
Was as long,
That a song
Was as merry,
That a cherry
Was as red—
That lead
Was as weighty
That fourscore
Was as eighty,
That a door
Was as wooden
   As in England—
So he stood in his shoes
   And he wondered,
   He wondered,
He stood in his shoes
   And he wondered.

John Keats

114

I WENT DOWN TO THE RIVER

I went down to the river
And I couldn't get across,

So I jumped on a mule—
I thought he was a horse.

The mule wouldn't pull,
So I traded him for a bull.

The bull wouldn't holler,
So I sold him for a dollar.

The dollar wouldn't pass,
So I threw it in the grass.

The grass wouldn't grow,
So I traded it for a hoe.

The hoe wouldn't dig,
So I traded it for a pig.

The pig wouldn't squeal,
So I traded it for a wheel.

The wheel wouldn't run,
So I traded it for a gun.

The gun wouldn't shoot,
So I traded it for a boot.

The boot wouldn't fit,
So I threw it in a pit,
And you fell in on it.

THERE WAS A TREE

There was a tree stood in the ground,
The prettiest tree you ever did see;
The tree in the wood, and the wood in the ground,
And the green grass grew all around,
And the green grass grew all around.

And on this tree there was a limb,
The prettiest limb you ever did see;
The limb on the tree, and the tree in the wood,
The tree in the wood, and wood in the ground,
And the green grass grew all around,
And the green grass grew all around.

And on this limb there was a bough,
The prettiest bough you ever did see;
The bough on the limb, and the limb on the tree,
The limb on the tree, and the tree in the wood,
The tree in the wood, and the wood in the ground,
And the green grass grew all around,
And the green grass grew all around.

116

Now on this bough there was a nest,
The prettiest nest you ever did see;
The nest on the bough, and the bough on the limb,
The bough on the limb, and the limb on the tree,
The limb on the tree, and the tree in the wood,
The tree in the wood, and the wood in the ground,
And the green grass grew all around,
And the green grass grew all around.

And in the nest there were some eggs,
The prettiest eggs you ever did see;
Eggs in the nest, and the nest on the bough,
The nest on the bough, and the bough on the limb,
The bough on the limb, and the limb on the tree,
The limb on the tree, and the tree in the wood,
The tree in the wood, and the wood in the ground,
And the green grass grew all around,
And the green grass grew all around.

GIDDY, GIDDY GOUT

Giddy, giddy Gout,
Your shirttail's out.
Three miles in
And three miles out.
If you don't put it in,
I'll tell Mrs. Snout.

OLD ROGER IS DEAD

Old Roger is dead and he lies
  in his grave,
They planted an apple tree
  over his head.
The apples got ripe and they
  fell to the ground
There came an old lady a-
  picking them up
Old Roger got up and gave
  her a thump.

TIDDLEDEE WINKS

Tiddledee Winks,
Tiddledee Winks,
Tiddledee Winks, the barber
Went to shave his father.
The razor slipped and cut his lip
And made the old man roar.
He upped with his fist and give
  him a blip,
And knocked Tiddledee Winks
  on the floor.

AS I WAS STANDING

As I was standing on the street,
  As quiet as can be,
A great big ugly man came up,
  And tied his horse to me.

A MAN OF WORDS

A man of words and not of deeds
Is like a garden full of weeds;
And when the weeds begin to grow,
It's like a garden full of snow;
And when the snow begins to fall,
It's like a bird upon the wall;
And when the bird away does fly,
It's like an eagle in the sky;
And when the sky begins to roar,
It's like a lion at the door;
And when the door begins to crack,
It's like a stick upon your back;
And when your back begins to smart,
It's like a penknife in your heart;
And when your heart begins to bleed,
You're dead, and dead, and dead, indeed.

HELLO, SIR

"Hello, hello, hello, sir,
Meet me at the grocer."
"No sir."
"Why sir?"
"Because I have a cold, sir."
"Where did you get your cold, sir?"
"At the North Pole, sir."
"What were you doing there, sir?"
"Shooting polar bear, sir."
"Let me hear you sneeze, sir."
"Kachoo, kachoo, kachoo, sir."

THE FOLK WHO LIVE IN BACKWARD TOWN

The folk who live in Backward Town
Are inside out and upside down.
They wear their hats inside their heads
And go to sleep beneath their beds.
They only eat the apple peeling
And take their walks across the ceiling.

Mary Ann Hoberman

119

THE NORTH WIND DOTH BLOW

The north wind doth blow,
And we shall have snow,
And what will the robin do then,
 poor thing?
He'll sit in a barn,
And keep himself warm,
And hide his head under his wing,
 poor thing!

The north wind doth blow,
And we shall have snow,
And what will the swallow do
 then, poor thing?
Oh, do you not know
That he's off long ago,
To a country where he will find
 spring, poor thing!

The north wind doth blow,
And we shall have snow,
And what will the dormouse do
 then, poor thing?
Roll'd up like a ball,
In his nest snug and small,
He'll sleep till warm weather
 comes in, poor thing!

The north wind doth blow,
And we shall have snow,
And what will the honey-bee do
 then, poor thing?
In his hive he will stay
Till the cold is away,
And then he'll come out in the
 spring, poor thing!

The north wind doth blow,
And we shall have snow,
And what will the children do
 then, poor things?
When lessons are done,
They must skip, jump, and run,
Until they have made themselves
 warm, poor things!

ALL THE PRETTY LITTLE HORSES

Hush-a-bye, hush-a-bye,
All the sleepy little babies,
When you wake, you will have cake,
And all the pretty little horses.

Black and bay, dapple and gray
Coach and six white horses.

Hush-a-bye, don't you cry,
Go to sleepy little baby,
When you wake, you will have cake,
And all the pretty little horses.

Way down yonder, down in the meadow
There's a poor little lambie,
The bees and butterflies buzzing 'round
    its eyes
Poor little thing crying Mammy.

Hush-a-bye, hush-a-bye,
Go to sleepy, little baby.
When you wake, you will have cake
And all the pretty little horses.

NEW MOON TELL ME

New moon, new moon,
Pray tell me
Who my true love is to be—
The color of his hair,
The clothes that he will wear,
And the day that we'll wedded be.

THE MOON SHINES BRIGHT

The moon shines bright,
The stars give a light,
And you may kiss
A pretty girl
At ten o'clock at night.

GO TO BED LATE

Go to bed late,
Stay very small.
Go to bed early,
Grow very tall.

BEDTIME

When Polly yelled, "I won't go to bed!"
This is what her mother said:

"I don't care if you don't go to bed!
I don't care if you turn off the light!
I don't care if you brush your teeth!
I don't care if you're up all night!
I don't care if you're tired in the morning!
I don't care if you're awake till then!
I don't care if you get your rest!
I don't care if you ever sleep again!"

Since Polly found this all quite boring,
She fell asleep and started snoring.

Jeff Moss

THE MOON SEES SOMEBODY

I see the moon,
The moon sees me.
The moon sees somebody,
That I want to see.

TWINKLE, TWINKLE, LITTLE BAT

Twinkle, twinkle, little bat!
How I wonder what you're at!
Up above the world you fly,
Like a tea-tray in the sky.
Twinkle, twinkle—

Lewis Carroll

I SEE THE MOON

I see the moon,
And the moon sees me.
God bless the moon,
And God bless me.

A PRAYER

Now I lay me down to sleep,
A bag of peanuts at my feet.
If I should die before I wake,
Give them to my sister Kate.

MISS POLLY HAD A DOLLY

Miss Polly had a dolly that was
  sick, sick, sick.
So she sent for the doctor
  quick, quick, quick.
The doctor came with his bag
  and hat
He knocked at the door with a
  Rat tat tat.

He looked at Miss Dolly and
  shook his head,
He said, "Miss Polly, put her
  straight to bed."
He wrote on some paper for a
  pill, pill, pill.
"I'll be back in the morning with the
  bill, bill, bill."

LIST OF POETS